Praise for Kate Saunders

Beswitched

"One of the most enchanting, funny and suspenseful
stories for 9+ to have been published for some time.
Pure bliss. Don't miss it"
Amanda Craig, *The Times*

"Magic ... time travel ... a funny and touching story...
This book has it all"
Eva Ibbotson

"Just occasionally you read a children's book that sweeps you so
entirely into its world that you leave your adult self behind"
Sunday Telegraph

"Combines wit and charm with hidden depths"
Observer

Magicalamity

"An action-packed romp ... Saunders serves up a deeply
plotted, satisfying blend of laughs and thrills"
Financial Times

"Great... Alan Bennett meets the Brothers Grimm"
The Sunday Times

"Kate Saunders is at her funny, fascinating, fast-pa
Scotsman

Kate Saunders has written lots of books
for adults and children. She lives in London.

Also by Kate Saunders

The Curse of the Chocolate Phoenix
The Whizz Pop Chocolate Shop
Magicalamity

The Belfry Witches
The Belfry Witches Fly Again
Cat and the Stinkwater War
The Little Secret

Beswitched

KATE SAUNDERS

MARION LLOYD BOOKS

First published in the UK in 2010 by Marion Lloyd Books
An imprint of Scholastic Children's Books
Euston House, 24 Eversholt Street
London, NW1 1DB, UK
A division of Scholastic Ltd
Registered office: Westfield Road, Southam, Warwickshire, CV47 0RA
SCHOLASTIC and associated logos are trademarks and/or registered
trademarks of Scholastic Inc.

This edition published 2013

Copyright © Kate Saunders, 2010
The right of Kate Saunders to be identified as the author
of this work has been asserted by her.

ISBN 9781407137315

A CIP catalogue record for this book is available
from the British Library

Printed and bound by CPI Group (UK) Ltd, Croydon, CR0 4YY
Papers used by Scholastic Children's Books are made from
wood grown in sustainable forests.

1 3 5 7 9 10 8 6 4 2

www.scholastic.co.uk/zone

For Joanna

Contents

Rock Bands
and Ponies

"At least look at the picture!" Flora's dad begged. "Don't you want to know what to expect?"

He pushed the glossy brochure across the table. It had a photo on the cover of a large white house on a very green lawn, and the words "Penrice Hall – Individual Fulfilment in a Home-like Atmosphere".

Flora scowled and pushed it back. "It doesn't matter what I expect, does it? Not unless I have a choice about going there."

Her father opened his mouth to say something, but her mother gently touched his arm to stop him.

"All he means," she told Flora, "is that you might like it."

"Well, I won't," Flora said. "Nothing on earth could make me like it."

1

Dad let out a long sigh that was half a groan. He looked anxious and exhausted, and even more ancient than usual – he had not had time to shave that morning, and the bristles on his chin were grey. The fact that he was a million years older than everyone else's dad had always been an embarrassment to Flora. Her mother, though not such a relic, also looked annoyingly old.

Flora was angry with them. Why couldn't they fix this disaster? Why were they being such wimps? They kept saying sorry – but what good was that when they refused to change anything?

"I need another coffee," Dad said, standing up. "Flora, do you want anything else? Another croissant?"

"No!" Flora snapped. "Stop trying to stuff me with food – do you want me to be fat as well as miserable?"

"We're fine," Mum assured him. "Don't rush, darling. There's plenty of time."

They were in a coffee shop at the station. Flora's gleaming new backpack and laptop case lay at her feet. Dad went to join the long queue at the counter.

"Plenty of time," Mum muttered again, looking at her watch. "I really think we'll be fine – though we're going to have to dash for our plane after we've seen you off." She leaned across the table. "Flora, please don't be so hard on Dad – he's having such a horrible time at the moment."

"*He's* having a horrible time! What about *me*?"

2

Flora's voice was tight with fury. "My entire life has just been destroyed!"

"Don't exaggerate."

"I've been separated from all my friends – my house is being torn apart—"

"Flora!" For the first time, her mother's voice had a hint of snap. "We're both desperately sorry about this whole situation – but there isn't a thing we can do about it – so don't you think you should start trying to accept it?"

"No!" Flora said. "Why do I have to go to a boarding school?"

"I've told you a million times," Mum said, obviously straining to be patient. "We don't know how long we're going to have to stay in Italy – or how long the builders are going to be at home – this is the only way we can cope. And it's only for two terms at the most."

"Why d'you have to go to Italy?"

"Stop it, Flora. You know perfectly well why – because Granny broke her hip and can't take care of herself. And because we've got to sell her house and about a hundred years' worth of furniture. And Lord knows when the new flat will be ready at our own house. Why must you make it more difficult? Are you really so selfish that you're making all this fuss about two terms at a boarding school? A very luxurious and expensive boarding school, I might add."

3

The unfairness of this was so enormous that it took Flora's breath away. "You and Dad are the selfish ones. You just decided everything without asking me."

Her mother suddenly looked very tired. "OK – what would you have done differently?"

This was even more unfair. Knowing what to do was their job. "I don't see why Granny has to come and live with us."

"She's your dad's mother and she's alone," Mum said. "All her husbands are either dead or married to other people. She's old and frail, and she can't look after herself. Where else is she supposed to go?"

"How should I know?" Flora snapped. "Can't he put her in a home?"

"*Flora!*"

Flora knew how nasty she sounded, but the misery of the past few days weighed on her chest like a stone. If she hadn't kept up being angry, she might have cried. "Dad doesn't even like Granny," she said bitterly.

"Don't be silly."

"She deserted him when he was little. She just ran away with her lover." Flora was scornful.

Mum sighed. "Well, yes, she did. Her lover was a very famous artist – and she got rather famous for inspiring him."

"For sleeping with him, you mean."

"Don't let Dad hear you talking like that."

4

"Why not?" Flora muttered. "Why can't I tell the truth all of a sudden?"

Mum sighed again, and frowned with the effort of choosing her words. "Look. Granny's not the maternal type – some women are like that. And Dad says he's glad he did all his growing up with his father and stepmother – you remember Nana, and how he adored her. He didn't get to know his real mother until he was in his twenties."

Flora had heard this story many times. "I know, I know – when he hitchhiked to Italy and turned up on her doorstep."

"He's very proud of her," Mum said firmly. "And you should be too – you're named after her, and she's a fascinating woman. The headmaster at Penrice Hall was really impressed when he heard that your granny was Flora Arditti. Lots of the kids at the school have famous parents, but I doubt you can go and see paintings of them in the National Portrait Gallery."

"Nude paintings," Flora pointed out. Famous pictures of your granny in the nude – how embarrassing was that?

"She's met everyone from Winston Churchill to Mick Jagger – Picasso painted her portrait. In her day she was one of the most beautiful women in Europe. She's practically a legend, and you should be glad you're getting this chance to know her properly."

"Well, I'm not." Flora was sick of hearing how "fascinating" and "wonderful" Granny was. "I've seen enough of her to know I don't like her. She's spooky and mean and always telling me off. That's what my life's going to be like from now on, isn't it? Nag, nag, nag. Brush your hair. Sit up straight. Stop texting at the table."

"Hmmm, yes," Mum said, "you've had it pretty easy up to now, I suppose." And she looked at Flora in a distant, thoughtful way, as if seeing her for the first time. "We've run the house around you."

"Are you saying I'm spoiled?"

"Well, no," Mum said doubtfully. "But you are rather used to getting your own way – and so is Granny. This isn't going to be easy for her, don't forget. She's used to having her own big house all to herself. A granny flat in a Wimbledon semi might seem like a bit of a comedown."

Flora said, "I can't do it, that's all. Italy was bad enough."

She suddenly had a vivid memory of Casa Boffi, her grandmother's big house in Italy, where she had spent two dreary weeks last summer. It was a dark and dusty place, in the middle of baking countryside, with no swimming pool for miles. The furniture was weird, and there were paintings everywhere. It had been like staying in a really hot, uncomfortable art gallery. There had been long, long meals, where Granny told endless stories about her four husbands and countless lovers.

A single tear slid down Flora's nose. It had been horrible. Flora had been allowed to bring her best friend, Ella, as company. Granny had barely noticed they were there – Mum had to cough loudly to remind her, when her stories got too rude. When she did notice, she forgot their ages and tried to give them gin and tonic.

"Which one is my grandchild again?" she had asked Dad one evening. "Is it the lumpy one or the little weasel?"

Ella was now her ex-best friend, and hadn't really spoken to her since. Flora had been furious about the "little weasel", and she didn't blame Ella for being angry with Granny for calling her "lumpy" – but why was Ella angry with *her*? She had tried and tried to put it right, but Ella carried on avoiding her. It had spoiled the first term at APS (short for Alderman Popham Secondary), which should have been so much fun.

And now her grandmother had to slip on a squashed grape and break her hip. The Italian mansion was too much for her to manage now, so Dad had decided to convert their garage in south London into a small flat. The scary old woman hung over them like a shadow.

Flora said, "I feel as if I've lost my home."

Mum reached across the table to squeeze her hand.

"My precious, try not to worry too much. Even if she wanted to, Granny couldn't turn a semi in Wimbledon into a copy of the Casa Boffi. We'll all have some adjusting to do."

Flora said, "But now I've got to face the boarding school. It's going to be a nightmare."

"Honestly, darling, Penrice Hall is incredibly relaxed and easy-going – you'll have your own little room – I think you're allowed to do your own cooking and phone out for takeaways – there's an Olympic-sized pool – five rock bands—"

"Blah-blah-blah-blah," Flora said rudely.

"Ponies—"

"It's no use, Mum. I know I'm going to hate it."

"Well then, you'll just have to hate it," Mum said.

There was a throb of anger in her voice that Flora recognized. When she was three she had screamed and screamed until she was finally allowed to wear a leotard to nursery in January. In exactly the same voice, Mum had said, "Well then, you'll just have to catch pneumonia."

Flora had learned then that no amount of screaming could make a January morning less cold. Her parents obeyed most of her wishes, but they couldn't change the weather or prevent old ladies from breaking their hips. They were going to Italy for three months, and she was going to the terrible school, and that was that.

"Oh bum," said Flora. "Fart and bum."

"Stop being so negative."

"I really will, you know. I really will totally hate it. For one thing, I'll be literally miles from everyone I know in the world."

Dad came back to the table and caught the end of this. "But you'll have your phone, darling. You'll be able to talk to us any time you like, day or night. And send us emails."

"It's not the same," said Flora. "And anyway, it won't do me much good. If I hate it you won't take me away."

"Yes, but you might not hate it. Penrice Hall is a famous school. We're lucky they had a place."

"Dad, please. I've just had this conversation with Mum. Spare me the rock bands and ponies."

The three of them spent the next few minutes in miserable silence. Flora looked at her reflection in the mirror on the opposite wall. She definitely did not look like a little weasel. But if only she didn't look so short and *young* – Yasmin, who was (sort of) her new best friend, looked at least fourteen. Still, the blonde streaks in her light brown hair added a bit of sophistication, and her new clothes were amazing. Her parents felt so guilty about sending her away that Mum had finally stopped trying to dress her in little skirts and flowery cardigans like a six-year-old, and let her choose exactly what she wanted – today, black jeans, red Converses, red T-shirt, silver belt and a seriously cool leather jacket.

Dad gulped his tiny cup of black coffee. He really did look crumbly this morning, Flora thought crossly. It was his own fault, for waiting so long to get married and have a baby. People sometimes thought he was Flora's grandad. He was so old that he had been born in 1950. If he wasn't so old, his mother wouldn't be such a dinosaur.

A large pigeon pecked at the crumbs on the floor. Station announcements boomed foggily overhead.

"That's us," Dad said. "Platform Seven." He leapt up and grabbed Flora's suitcase – almost as if he were relieved to be getting rid of her.

Two huge cases had already been sent ahead by Red Star – cases crammed with wonderful new clothes, make-up and books. Flora only had her snazzy new backpack containing her iPod and the small case for her laptop. Flora had to admit that there were some good things about going away to boarding school. Yasmin had even confessed that she was jealous – "I'd go to army boot camp if it meant I got a new laptop."

But Yasmin didn't understand how it felt to be let down by your parents. Flora's selfish parents thought they were angels because they wouldn't put Granny in a home – even though she was a notoriously tough old lady who might even have liked it. Yet they saw nothing wrong with banishing their sensitive daughter. She was determined not to let them think they had been forgiven.

"There's no need to get on the train with me," she told her dad haughtily.

As usual, her parents ignored her and climbed on to the train with her like two clucking old hens.

Dad put her laptop case on the small table. "Now, darling, the train manager knows you're an unaccompanied minor, and he'll—"

"Dad, stop telling me. That's the billionth time this morning."

Mum handed her a posh tuna baguette. "He'll make sure you get off at the right station—"

"I'm not a baby," Flora said crossly. "I know where to get off."

"—and you'll be met by Fiona, who's one of the teachers at Penrice Hall."

"Any problems, just call us," Dad said. "Call us whenever you like."

"Oh, my darling –" Mum hugged her hard – "I'm going to miss you so much!"

Dad said, "Bye-bye, bunny rabbit," and gave her another big hug.

And then the whistle shrieked, and they had to leave her.

Flora did not like this moment at all. Suddenly, seeing her parents on the other side of the glass made her feel very young and very lonely. They waved as the train pulled out of the station and bravely tried to smile – though they obviously felt more like crying.

Suddenly, all she remembered was how much she loved the foolish old things, and she blew kisses at them for as long as she could see them – and then there was a massive lump in her throat. But there were other people in the carriage, and Flora did not want them to think she was pathetic – the "bunny rabbit" Dad had let slip was embarrassing enough. She sniffed a couple of times and stared out of the window, until there was no more danger of breaking down.

After this, she found that she felt fine. A woman came round with a trolley, and Flora bought herself a bottle of apple juice. There was something rather elegant and mature about travelling alone, she decided. The train was going so fast that the nearest houses and gardens slipped by in a silent blur. Now that her parents were no longer watching her, Flora could take a proper look at the brochure for Penrice Hall.

The big white house, she had to admit, didn't look at all bad. Inside the brochure, there was a photo of a man with a beard. "Hi, I'm Jeff, the headmaster," said the text underneath. "Here at Penrice, we believe education should be tailored to the individual. Young people know instinctively what they need to learn, and our students are encouraged to draw up their own timetables. A Penrice teacher is a good mate – not an authority figure!" There were pictures of a swimming pool, a pottery shed and a music studio, all thronged with grinning kids in cool clothes. If it really looked like this, the place might be all right.

She had meant to send a text to Yasmin – something like "This sux!" – but Yasmin wasn't such a good best friend as Ella had been. Suddenly, Flora felt desperately tired. She barely had time to wonder why before a great wave of sleep crashed over her.

A voice was speaking very close to her ear – so close that Flora heard it deep inside her head. It was the voice of a girl, solemn and clear.

> *"We summon you! Come to us! We summon you!*
> *From the far north of the years to come!*
> *With hare's whisker,*
> *With hog's bristle,*
> *With two sprigs of milk thistle,*
> *A stone from the stream's rush,*
> *A hair from the fox's brush!"*

She knew it was not a real voice. She was in the middle of a dream.

It was pitch dark. Flora tried to open her eyes, but her eyelids felt as heavy as two metal shutters.

Then, while her eyes were still tightly shut, she saw it all.

She was in a dark room lit by two misty smears of candlelight. She did not know why she was there, except that she had somehow obeyed the mysterious summons.

There were three figures draped in white — like ghosts in a cartoon. Did they want to scare her? Flora tried to concentrate harder on this dream, so that she could see them more clearly. If the white shapes had arms, they seemed to be waving them. There was an odd noise — like loud screams heard from very far away.

Flora was not scared. She felt quite calm. She could see a large window, with long, blue-patterned curtains on either side. One of the spirits began to move towards her, and Flora felt herself being pulled away — not painfully, but very firmly. The dark room with the white figures suddenly vanished, like a candle being blown out.

She was flying now, or perhaps falling. It was like being sucked back into a gigantic vacuum cleaner. She could see nothing but darkness. A great whirlpool of sounds was babbling inside her head — voices and engines, explosions, crowds cheering. She was flying faster than the wind.

It did not last long. Flora felt herself gasping as she was suddenly thrown out of the dream and poured back into her sleeping body on the train.

But something was wrong. Her arms and legs seemed to be wrapped in thick, soft layers of cloth. Her feet had landed in shoes that were hard and heavy.

"Flora," a woman's voice said. "Wake up, dear. We're nearly there."

2
Changing Trains

This was not a dream. Flora was sure she was not dreaming now. She struggled to open her sleep-swollen eyes. Who had spoken to her as if they knew her? Where was she? Yes, she was on a train — but a different train. It swung and creaked and clattered, with a regular rhythm — ta-ta-ta-TUM, ta-ta-ta-TUM — that made her thoughts march in time to it like soldiers.

The light was dim and yellow. It came from two funny little lamps in the wall. She was in a compartment with a sliding door. Outside the window were grey hills that were fading into darkness. On the wall underneath the luggage rack was a small framed picture of a sunny beach, and the words, "PAIGNTON – England's Summer Playground".

Flora looked down at her own arm, and her heart did a somersault of shock. Instead of her long-sleeved T-shirt, she appeared to be wearing a dark green jacket. Something was throttling her neck uncomfortably – a green tie with red stripes, like the tie her dad wore to his office. How did it get there? She had never worn a tie in her life. Had she been knocked out and kidnapped and forced into someone else's clothes? No, don't be silly.

"Come along, come along!" said the strange voice. "Dear me, we are a sleepy owl today!"

There was one other person in the compartment. It was a solid, shapeless woman, with neat rolls of brown hair under a brown felt hat, and glasses with heavy brown frames. Flora could not tell how old she was. At first glance, she looked older than Mum because her clothes were so old-fashioned. When you looked more closely, however, her beaming face was round and fresh. She was wearing a man's tweed suit with a collar and tie, except that instead of trousers the suit had a long stiff skirt. Her shoes were clumpy brown lace-ups. She was reading a magazine called *Time and Tide*. Flora's heart was thumping hard. Something very strange and terrible was happening, and her brain was too stunned with shock to take it in.

She croaked, "Where am I?"

"You fell asleep, dear," the woman said, "that's all.

I'm not surprised that you're tired – you've had a long journey today."

"Long?" Flora echoed. She had only come from Wimbledon, and the journey had hardly started. She did not understand. This woman obviously thought she was someone else – but who?

"Why don't you run along the corridor," the woman suggested, "and splash your face with some water?"

She went back to reading her magazine, as if nothing unusual had happened.

Flora stood up, suddenly eager to get out of the compartment, still wildly hoping things would somehow get back to normal. Once she had pulled open the sliding door, however, and stepped out into the corridor, she saw that the entire train belonged to the new and baffling world.

All the compartments were filled with oddly dressed people. Every single woman wore a hat. The men wore heavy suits and stiff collars. Many people were smoking. Flora saw one man puffing on a pipe. The air was dim and reeking with smoke. It swirled in blue columns around the lights. Nobody seemed to think this might be unhealthy.

The toilet door was made of heavy wood, and said "WC". Flora darted inside and shot the bolt. Her head felt muddled and woolly, and she needed to think. If this was not a dream, there had to be some rational explanation.

Hallucination? Reality television? An elaborate joke?

There was a gleaming white basin, with brass taps. The lavatory was solid and throne-like. A cool wind knifed in through the frosted window, and Flora's mind felt a little sharper. She turned, and jumped to see her own face gazing back at her in the small mirror above the basin.

It's me, she thought – *but it's not me*.

The Flora in the mirror had light brown hair cut into a short, neat bob with a side parting – a hairstyle worn by nobody over the age of three. And where were her fabulous blonde streaks? Where were the holes for her earrings? Somehow, as part of the general horror, her ears had become unpierced. She had been turned into a freak. She looked like a little girl!

Feverishly – longing for a full-length mirror – Flora examined her clothes. Under the green jacket she was wearing a hideous black pinafore dress with boxy pleats all the way down. It was tied at the waist with a belt of bright orange. Underneath the pinafore was a scratchy white shirt, with the stiff collar and striped tie.

And underneath that—

"*Bum!*" whispered Flora.

Her underwear was unbelievable. Under the shirt, she was wearing a mad vest. It was very long and it had straps fixed to the hem. These straps held up thick

19

brown stockings. Worst of all, over the vest-and-stockings thing, she was wearing huge, baggy, dark green knickers, with elasticated legs that came halfway down to her knees. One of the legs had a cotton handkerchief tucked into the elastic.

Though she was alone, Flora blushed hotly with embarrassment.

Thank goodness none of my friends can see me, she thought – *I'd never hear the last of these comedy bloomers.*

It felt odd to be wearing so many layers of clothes, like a pass-the-parcel at a party. She wondered what to do next. Phoning for help was impossible – she didn't have a phone any more, and she had a strong feeling that mobile phones were unheard of in this weird new world. So were laptops and iPods, she suspected. She didn't even have her own watch any more – the new one was very plain, on a brown leather strap, and obviously didn't do anything except tell the time.

She used the royal lavatory. It was so high that her feet did not touch the ground when she sat down. There was a little notice beside it, which said, "Passengers Will Please Refrain from Pulling the Chain While the Train is at a Station".

Flora pulled the chain, and for a moment was distracted by the sight of a flap opening at the bottom of the toilet bowl and suddenly showing the ground rushing past beneath them.

Her parents would be worried sick when she didn't call. But how could she get in touch with them? How could they rescue her? Her stomach lurched with fear. She had a horrible, sick certainty that there was no way on earth her parents would ever find her here — wherever "here" might be. She didn't even know how she should ask for help. Because there was nothing else she could do, Flora hurried back to the woman who seemed to know her. She was still hoping someone would explain.

In the compartment, the woman was lifting two brown leather suitcases from the luggage rack. Flora was surprised and confused to see her own name — Flora Fox — on the labels. Perhaps, she thought desperately, this is all something to do with Penrice Hall, and this woman is Fiona, and I've lost my short-term memory—

"Here you are," said the woman who might be Fiona. "Poor thing, you're awfully pale." She handed Flora a hat made of dark green felt, with a ribbon round it that matched the striped tie. "We're going have a breezy drive in my car, so you'd better put on your mackintosh."

"My — what?"

"Do try to wake up, Flora." The woman swept a bulky green coat off the seat. "Your school mac."

Flora struggled into the coat and put on the hat. The

train was lurching and shuddering to a halt. Clouds of steam hissed up outside the window.

"And don't forget your hockey stick!" The strange woman pushed a hockey stick into Flora's hand. "I wish you'd managed to eat something – you're as white as a little ghost, and you've missed lower-school tea."

"I think there's been a mistake," Flora said. "Are you from Penrice Hall?"

"Come along. Best foot forward." The woman strode out of the compartment, swinging the two heavy cases as if they had been filled with feathers.

Flora hurried after her, down the corridor and out of the train. The evening air was cold on her face. Along the platform, a whistle shrilled. The train pulled out of the station – puffing loudly, like Thomas the Tank Engine – and away into deep silence. This was a very small station, marooned in a great lonely sea of dark nothingness.

Out of the darkness a figure appeared. It was a brisk old man in a peaked cap and little round glasses, whose mouth was invisible behind a large grey moustache. He wheeled two big wooden boxes on a trolley. In the gleam of light from the windows of the station building, Flora saw her own name painted on the boxes.

"Evening, Miss Bradley," said the old man.

So this was the name of the woman in the suit.

"Good evening, Watkins," said Miss Bradley.

"I thought your girls all came back yesterday."

"Flora is starting a day late," Miss Bradley said. "Her parents sailed out to India this morning."

"Oh, no – that's wrong," Flora said quickly. "They've only flown to Italy, and I think there's been—"

"It'll be at least another two years before she sees them again," Miss Bradley added.

"Two years? Oh no, that's completely wrong! They're only staying for a few months!" Flora meant to speak very firmly, but her voice refused to obey her brain and came out as a toothless burble.

"She's dog-tired, poor little thing," Miss Bradley told Watkins, as if she had not heard. "And no wonder, when she's come all the way from Southampton."

"But I haven't!" Flora protested. "I've come from London, and there's been a terrible—"

"I met her at Paddington," Miss Bradley went on. She took a cigarette out of a packet that said "Sweet Afton", and deftly lit it with a match she struck on the bottom of her shoe. "And she's been jolly brave, I must say."

Watkins looked at Flora, and his moustache stretched into a friendly grin. "That's the spirit, Miss. Keep smiling."

Flora said, "I'm sorry, I think there's been a mistake. I think you might be taking me to the wrong school."

This time, Miss Bradley heard. She chuckled kindly. "I've been at St Winifred's for eight years – I ought to know where it is by now. And I do assure you, we've been expecting you for weeks."

"Are you from Penrice Hall?"

"What on earth are you talking about?" Miss Bradley blew out a plume of smoke and looked at Flora more closely. "I'm from St Winifred's, you poor addled child, and that's where we'll be in about half an hour – if my car behaves herself."

Watkins said, "I topped up the radiator, Miss B."

"Watkins, you're a trump. Will you bring the boxes up to the school when you come off duty?"

"Right you are, Miss." He touched the peak of his cap.

An idea struck Flora like lightning – she was amazed she hadn't thought of it sooner. "Of course!" she cried. "I know this sounds crazy – but it all fits! If this really isn't a dream, I've travelled back in time! I'm in the past!"

Miss Bradley chuckled. "My dear child! You're absolutely drunk with sleep! You need a good blast of fresh air."

"What year is this?"

"Don't be nonsensical."

"Please! What year is this? Where am I?"

"Don't worry, you haven't slipped into a novel by

H.G. Wells," Miss Bradley said cheerfully. "You're still in good old 1935."

The hockey stick slipped out of Flora's grasp and clattered to the ground.

She whispered, "Oh — bum."

3
Old Peepy

Flora picked up her hockey stick and followed Miss Bradley (who had fortunately not heard the rude word), because there was nothing else she could do. If she really had somehow landed in 1935, it would be no use trying to call her parents – with a shiver, she realized they had not been born yet.

They left the station by a wooden gate. A single lamp on the wall shed feeble light on a very small car parked out in the lane. It had a dent in the bonnet and looked about as sturdy as a biscuit tin. Flora climbed in beside Miss Bradley. There were no seat belts. The seats were very low, and her bum was only about six inches above the road. It couldn't be safe.

She wondered what would happen if she died in a

car crash in the past – would she get born again at the right time? If so, would she then travel back in time again, and die again? And then get born again? She mustn't think about this, she decided, or her thoughts would drive her crazy.

They hurtled along black lanes and around terrifying blind corners. In the beam of the headlights, Flora glimpsed high hedgerows, low branches, and single lighted windows suspended in the darkness. Miss Bradley did not seem to have heard of speed limits.

After a hairy half-hour of her breakneck driving, they suddenly swerved through a huge pair of iron gates and along a short avenue of trees. The car stopped with a jolt outside an enormous square white house.

"And here we are, sound in wind and limb." Miss Bradley jumped out of the car. "Out you get, Flora – welcome to St Winifred's."

Flora struggled out of the car. The great house had rows of long lighted windows. Behind the windows, she could hear the unmistakable sounds of a school – laughter, voices calling, feet thumping on stairs, crockery clinking, two pianos and a violin all playing different tunes.

For the first time since the beginning of this nightmare, Flora relaxed enough to look around with real interest. Without knowing why, she had a sense of being welcomed. When she walked through the big double doors at the top of the steps, the house greeted her with a kindly smell of warm dust, floor polish and custard.

Miss Bradley led her into a large entrance hall with a floor of black and white marble. There was a magnificent staircase of carved wood, and two neat noticeboards. A small coal fire burned in a huge marble fireplace. Above the fireplace was a grim portrait of a white-haired lady in a black gown.

"Our founder," Miss Bradley said. "Dame Mildred Beak – a great pioneer of women's education." She pressed what looked like a doorbell at the side of the fireplace.

A door opened under the stairs. A young woman came out, in a black dress and white apron, with a white cap on her head. Flora had seen enough television dramas to know that this must be a maid – a real maid, in a real, traditional maid's uniform. She was very young, and Flora thought she was pretty. She had snapping dark eyes, and a rosy, laughing face.

"Ethel," said Miss Bradley, "this is our new girl, Miss Flora Fox. Will you take her things up to her bedroom?"

"Yes, Miss," Ethel said. Behind Miss Bradley's back, she gave Flora the ghost of a wink.

"Come along, Flora – we don't want to keep the head waiting." Miss Bradley patted her shoulder. "Ethel, do take her hockey stick – and Flora, remove your hat and coat, dear. Chin up!"

28

Though she was so loud and jolly, Miss Bradley seemed to be a little afraid of the head. She smoothed Flora's hair and tugged at her collar. She muttered, "Speak when you're spoken to – and for the love of Mike, don't mention time travel!"

She knocked once on a door of gleaming dark wood.

"Enter!" cried a majestic voice.

Flora stood up as straight as she could and squared her shoulders. She could see that it was no use trying to make Miss Bradley understand her, or even listen to her, but it was vital that she made herself clear to the headmistress. There had been a mistake – a gigantic mistake, a cosmic mistake. Something had to be done about it.

Miss Bradley gently pushed her into the headmistress's room. It was large, with long windows from floor to ceiling, but this was not what Flora noticed first. The room was dominated by a great, gleaming, carved desk, which seemed to loom out of the lamplight like the prow of a ship.

Miss Bradley said, "Here's Flora Fox, Headmistress. She's rather tired, and she hasn't had a thing to eat. I'm afraid the parting upset her rather."

Flora stared across the desk at the head. Her dark grey hair was scraped into a bun at the back of her neck. Otherwise you would have thought she was a man. Just like Miss Bradley, she was wearing a suit with a collar and tie, and not one scrap of make-up. She seemed extremely old – as old and strong as a mountain, and equally remote.

"Yes, it's often hard," the headmistress said. "I've seen it so many times. Tell Ethel to bring her a plate of bread and butter and some tea."

"Yes, Headmistress." Miss Bradley gave Flora an encouraging smile and ducked out of the room.

The headmistress stood up and came round the desk. She was very tall, with the long, curved nose of a Roman emperor. Her eyebrows were like two hairy black and grey caterpillars. Flora tried not to stare – but didn't she have tweezers?

She shook Flora's hand. Her fingers felt cold and strong. "How do you do, Flora. I am Miss Powers-Prout – or, as the girls insist upon calling me behind my back, Old Peepy. Your father's letter informs me that you have never been away to school. I hope you will find St Winifred's a home from home."

"There's been a mistake," Flora blurted out. This time, she was determined to be heard. "My dad can't have written to you – I'm not meant to be here. I'm meant to be at Penrice Hall – I don't know exactly where it is, but the headmaster's called Jeff."

The words died in her mouth. Miss Powers-Prout was glaring down at her with a look on her face.

"I've got the brochure in my backpack," Flora

30

galloped on desperately. "I don't know where it's got to – my proper luggage just disappeared when I was on the train. I've lost my iPod and my laptop, and all my Jacqueline Wilson books, and these stupid clothes certainly don't belong to me—"

"I can see you've never been to school before," Miss Powers-Prout said. "At St Winifred's, Flora, little girls do not address their elders in that rude manner."

"But I'm not being rude! I'm only trying to explain what's happened! And you've got to listen to me!"

"I beg your pardon?"

"I've come to the wrong school! I'm expected at Penrice Hall!"

"Stop this nonsense at once!" snapped Miss Powers-Prout. "Good gracious – has no one taught you manners? That is something you will certainly learn while you are here. A St Winifred's girl is known for her ladylike demeanour. Politeness was enshrined in our rules by Dame Mildred Beak herself!"

Flora wanted to scream with frustration. Why would nobody listen to her? "Look, Miss Peepy, or whatever your name is, for the last time, I've been taken back into the past – I'm from way in the future – I don't even know if this is real or part of my dream – and I can't possibly stay at this stupid school!"

The awful speckled eyebrows pulled together in a frown. "That is quite enough, Flora. Foul language will

31

not be tolerated. If you had not just arrived, I should be forced to give you a black mark. Please be quiet."

"No!" Flora shouted. "Why should I? You can't tell me when to speak! Get me out of here! I want to go home!"

Suddenly, her senses were spinning again. Her mind was a pack of cards, and it was being violently shuffled. Memories shifted inside her head, and not all of them belonged to her — she remembered heat and dust, spices and elephants, a monkey named Fritz, and a brown lady in a sari whom she loved. Were these the memories of another Flora Fox — the one who had really been expected here? If so, what had happened to *her*? Was she sitting, at this very minute across time, in the study of Jeff at Penrice Hall?

It was hopeless. Her proper memories were running away from her, and the modern world where she belonged seemed as distant as a dream. Her heart ached with longing for Mum and Dad — and even there, the wrong memories kept getting in the way of the right ones. Had her mother ever worn a flowered hat? Had her father ever carried a rifle?

Flora felt like the loneliest person in the universe. All the fear and bewilderment of the day came rushing out of her in a storm of tears. She cried now as she had never cried in her life — she almost howled.

Miss Powers-Prout said, "T-t-t-t-t!" She put her arm

around Flora's heaving shoulders and steered her towards an armchair beside the fire. "Come now! Let's not give way! I know it's hard to say goodbye to your parents for such a long time. But don't you think they'd want you to be brave?" She gave Flora a handkerchief made of stiff white cotton.

There was a knock at the door.

"Enter!" cried Miss Powers-Prout.

Ethel came in, carrying a large tray. She put this down on the low table beside the fire. Flora made an effort to swallow her sobs. From behind the handkerchief she watched Ethel setting down pale blue cups and saucers, a plate of bread cut into triangles and a silver teapot.

"You will feel better," said Miss Powers-Prout, "when you have had something to eat. Thank you, Ethel."

Unseen by the headmistress, Ethel managed to give Flora's arm a reassuring squeeze. Flora was a little ashamed that Ethel had seen her tears, but her kindness was very comforting.

Miss Powers-Prout poured them both a cup of tea. She handed Flora the plate of white bread and butter. Flora was very hungry. She devoured the bread and butter – making an effort to do it politely because she couldn't face another lecture about manners. The bread tasted good, and so did the tea.

Miss Powers-Prout took the armchair on the other side of the fireplace. "I shall overlook your disgraceful exhibition just now, because I know how hard it is for girls whose people are in the colonies. We have quite a few such girls at St Winifred's, so you will not be alone."

Flora wondered if the "colonies" had something to do with ants.

Her bewilderment must have shown on her face. Miss Powers-Prout stopped frowning, and leaned across the low table to look at Flora more closely. Her eyes were black and brilliant under the thick grey brows. "Of course you miss your life in India – that is only to be expected, when you have never known anything else. But, Flora, your father writes that he wants you to know England, and learn to love its peculiar beauty – a somewhat cold, damp beauty, I must admit."

She stood up briskly and snapped on a lamp. It lit up a big map of the world on the wall behind it. "You must not feel, however, that you are far from home. As an English person, you are at home in every corner of the world." She pointed to the British Isles: a little patch of pink. "This is where you are now." Her hand moved across to India, also pink. "And this is where you came from. Think of all the pink countries as home."

34

Flora looked at the map. Most of the countries were pink. She remembered Ms Stuart, her history teacher in the twenty-first century, telling her that Britain had once ruled a lot of other countries. She wished she had paid more attention in Ms Stuart's lessons.

"That's the glory of the British Empire." Miss Powers-Prout switched off the lamp. "You are at home in every corner of the world. But England is the Empire's heart and soul, and your parents expect us to turn you into a real English schoolgirl. I will make every possible allowance for your inexperience, Flora – but I warn you now, I will not tolerate rudeness. While at this school, you will be polite and ladylike. You will work hard. Do I make myself understood?"

"Yes," Flora said.

"You will address me as Miss Powers-Prout."

Flora's face burned. She hated the way the old bag glared at her, but didn't want to set her off again. "Yes, Miss Powers-Prout."

"Good." The headmistress gave her a frosty smile. "I'm afraid you're the only new girl, since it's not the beginning of the school year – but I'm sure you'll soon settle in. It is already past lower-school bedtime. Your form prefect will show you to your dormitory."

4

The Bluebells

Flora left the head's study in despair.

I'm doomed, she thought – *nobody's ever going to believe me, and my real life feels so far off, I might as well have dreamed it.*

There was one other person in the deserted hall. A tall girl in school uniform waited beside the fireplace. She smiled at Flora. "Hello. You must be the maggot."

"The – what?" Flora's tired head swam. Despite the uniform, this girl looked too old to be at school. She was thin, with a sharp and rather sarcastic face, and a neat cap of dark hair.

"Don't take it personally," the tall girl added, "it only means you're new. I was a maggot once, if it's any consolation."

"Are you a – teacher?"

"Certainly not – I'm in the lower sixth, and I have the honour to be your form prefect." She held out her hand. "Virginia Denning."

Flora shook her hand. "Flora Fox."

"How do you do, Flora? It's only half an hour till lights out, so we'd better hurry up to your dorm." She started up the large staircase.

Flora had to scamper to keep up with her. "My what?"

"Your dormitory."

"You mean – I have to share with other people?"

Virginia was amused. "That's the general idea."

This was the last straw. Flora hated sharing a bedroom – except with Ella, who was no longer her best friend. "How many other people?"

"Three."

Flora groaned. "Three other people! And I suppose that means we have to share a bathroom?"

"I'm afraid so." Virginia looked over her shoulder. Her eyes were as green as grapes, smiling and quick behind her glasses. If she had worn contact lenses, and a little blusher on her pale cheeks, Flora thought, and done something about that old-lady hairstyle, she would have been pretty. "You've never been to school before, have you?"

"No."

"Of course, you're an Indian girl. Did you go to a day school out there?"

Flora could not tell Virginia about coming from the future. She decided to lie, but what came out felt true, and she even had memories to go with it. "I had a governess."

Whose name was Miss Foster; I shared her with the two girls next door and we had lessons on the veranda.

This was odd. Her brain kept darting off into the mind of another Flora, the girl whose life she had slipped into.

"I know exactly how you feel," Virginia said. "I stayed at home with a governess until I was twelve."

"Are you from India too?"

"No, we lived in Paris and Vienna. School came as a shock, to say the least. I was horrified by the lack of coffee, and the coarseness of the sheets."

"I have an en suite shower room at home," Flora said. "I like a hot shower every morning."

"Hmm, I'd better show you the cloakrooms for your floor – that's what we call bathrooms here." Virginia led Flora into a long corridor, lined with doors, and opened the first of the doors. Flora looked inside. There was a row of toilet cubicles and sinks. Facing this was another row of cubicles, each containing a bath – she could see because one of the doors was open, and there was a girl inside drying her hair with a towel. There was a strong smell of the stuff Mum used to clean the sink.

"Sorry, Cynthia – don't mind us," Virginia said. "I'm just giving the gen to the maggot. This is she."

"Hello," said the girl under the towel.

Virginia pulled Flora back into the corridor. "You get two baths a week – Wednesday and Saturday."

Flora felt slightly sick. Two baths a week! This was like prison. She stumbled after Virginia, trying not to start crying again.

Each door in the corridor had a flower name – Rose, Carnation, Iris, Eglantine. There was a babble of voices and giggles, and – from somewhere – loud shrieks.

Virginia halted in front of Bluebell. This was where the shrieks were coming from. Behind the door, Flora heard a girl's voice shouting, "Ow! Stoppit, you beast! OW! You utter putrid BEAST!"

"Charming," Virginia said calmly. She opened the door. Two girls were wrestling on the dormitory floor. When they saw Virginia, they scrambled to their feet. "If I were the cruel type of prefect," Virginia said, "and if I could be bothered, I'd deal out some hideous punishment. Wasn't the rumpus last night bad enough?"

The tallest of the girls mumbled, "Sorry, Virginia."

"I've brought you the new girl, Flora Fox. Try not to converse with her in bloodcurdling screams." She pulled Flora properly into the room. "Flora, meet your fellow Bluebells, Daphne Peterson, Cecilia Lawrence and Dulcie Latimer."

Each girl solemnly shook hands with Flora – there was a lot of handshaking in the past.

"Look after her, you three."

The three girls said, "Yes, Virginia."

This was a very strict school, Flora thought – or why did these three girls take orders so meekly, and from someone who wasn't even a member of staff?

"Don't forget, it's lights out in half an hour. Goodnight, Flora – it won't look so ghastly in the morning."

When Virginia had gone, the three girls stared in silence at Flora. She stared back, relieved to see that, despite their stupid uniforms and the yawning time-difference between them, they seemed to be as normal as anyone in her class at APS.

She looked round the room. It was large and pleasant, cheerfully lit. At first, Flora thought it was furnished with four large, flowered tents; then she saw that these were beds surrounded by curtains, like cubicles in a hospital. Each cubicle contained a bed with a metal frame, a chest of drawers and a bedside table with a lamp.

The tallest of the three girls said, "How do you do. I'm Pete."

Flora thought she must have heard wrong.

"My full name is Daphne Peterson – but I decided to call myself 'Pete' because 'Daphne' is so wet. My middle name is 'Flora', same as yours. But I didn't like that either."

Pete's hair was short and dark, and just curly enough to be in a constant state of untidiness. The first thing you noticed about Pete was her untidiness. Her school clothes had an air of hanging in tatters. Her tie was crooked, and her hands were stained with blobs of blue ink. In spite of this, however, there was something commanding in the way she held herself. Her eyes were of a piercing, fearless blue. They swept over Flora in a way that disturbed her to the marrow of her bones – she had no idea why. Could she have seen Pete's sharp features before? And if so, in whose life?

Pete patted the skinny shoulder of the girl beside her. "This is Pogo Lawrence."

"My brothers nicknamed me 'Pogo' when I was a baby," Pogo explained. "I've never managed to shake it off. Only my mother and Old Peepy call me 'Cecilia'." She was a couple of inches shorter than Flora, and she looked as wizened and wiry and tough as a little jockey.

The third girl said, "I'm just Dulcie. How do you do?"

Dulcie was plump and fair, pink and blooming. She had two long pale yellow plaits. Her eyes were huge and babyishly blue behind round glasses.

There was a silence. Flora felt that the other three girls were sizing her up.

"Your bed's the one nearest the door," Pete told her. "Sorry about that – it's the penalty of arriving last." She jerked back the curtain around Flora's bed. "You won't need to worry about unpacking your overnighter."

"My what?"

"You know. The small bag with your pyjamas and sponge bag – the things you'll need for tonight, before you unpack your boxes. Ethel did it for you. She's such a brick."

"She told us you were crying," Dulcie said solemnly, "because you were homesick."

Pogo said, "Your parents have gone back to India, haven't they? I know how rotten that feels. Mine are in Rangoon – my father's the Bishop of Burma."

Flora saw that the three girls wanted to be kind. For the first time since the transformation on the train, she was with people she could talk to as an equal – they might think she was crazy, but they couldn't lecture her or hand out order marks.

She took a deep breath. "My parents aren't in India. They've never even been to India. They're in the next century. That's where I come from. I live in Wimbledon in the twenty-first century. I've fallen under some kind of spell and travelled back in time. I was supposed to be going to a modern school called Penrice Hall, but I ended up here. You probably don't believe me, but I don't care. It's the truth."

The other three girls gaped. There was a silence.

"Oh-h-h-h!" quavered Dulcie.

"You mean . . ." Pete said, "you mean you're from – the future?"

"Yes."

"This is some kind of trick," Pogo said sourly. "Very funny."

Flora was very tired. She didn't have any more strength to argue. "I swear it's not a joke and it's not a trick. I had a mad dream on the train."

Their reaction was puzzling. She had expected them to laugh at her. Instead, they were pale and scared, and – in Pete's case – excited.

"Great snakes!" she whispered. "It worked!"

Dulcie's lips trembled. "Oh, Pete, I'm so scared!"

"Rubbish!" snapped Pogo. "She's not from the future – it's a trick!"

Flora looked around the room again, trying to work out what was niggling at her memory – then she saw it.

The curtains at the window and around the beds, patterned with bluebells, were the curtains she had seen in her dream.

5

The Summoning

"This is it!" Flora blurted out, almost choking with excitement. "This is where it happened!" The curtains were the same, the windows were the same. This was the same dark chamber Flora had seen in her dream. She sat down heavily on her bed. "I've been here before, when I was asleep on the train. There were some white shapes – someone screaming – and a voice – saying a poem about milk thistle and hog's bristle – and I think there were candles." She reddened slightly while she was saying all this – it sounded so barking mad.

But the other girls did not laugh at her, or argue. They stared at Flora like three statues of amazement. Dulcie began to cry.

"Wow," Flora said. "You believe me!"

"So we jolly well should," said Pete. "We're the ones who brought you here."

"You? What are you talking about?"

"Don't you see?" Pete turned eagerly to the others. "The ghostly figure we saw was HER! And she saw us!" She turned back to Flora. "We did it last night, because it was the first night back and we wanted something to cheer us up. We had sheets over our heads to get into the mood. The voice you heard saying the spell was mine—"

"And the screams were Dulcie's," Pogo said, with a dry chuckle. "She had the whole corridor in an uproar. We got into absolute oceans of hot water."

"I couldn't help it!" protested Dulcie. "I was so frightened! She was all transparent like a jellyfish!"

Flora's heart was beating so hard that she could hear it inside her ears. "But I don't understand – why did you do this? How did you? Why am I here?"

"Well, we summoned you," Pete said, rather grandly. She seemed very pleased with herself. "Crikey, this is thrilling – what was it like?"

At last, someone was really listening. Her words falling over each other, Flora poured out the whole story of her turbulent day. It took a long time, because the three girls kept interrupting.

"A laptop what?" asked Dulcie. "Is it a little table for having breakfast in bed?"

"Do you really carry your own telephones in the future?" asked Pogo. "Don't the wires get in the way?"

Pete asked, "Did your evil granny really have four husbands? How did they all die?"

"Look, I'll answer questions later," Flora said eventually. "I'm more or less at the end, but there's something else you should know – I think I've swapped places with another Flora Fox, whose parents really are in India. I keep having flashes of her memories. And she's probably having flashes of mine, wherever she might be. I don't want to go back to the future to find she's done something terrible while she was in my life."

A bell clanged loudly.

Pete groaned. "The ten-minute warning! Just when it's getting interesting!"

"We should get moving," Pogo said, pulling at her tie. "Harbottle's dying to give us another pony." Seeing Flora's bafflement, she added, "A 'pony' is what we call a black mark here – it's short for 'poena', which is Latin for 'penalty'."

"Oh." Flora tugged uncertainly at her tie. The other girls stripped off their complicated layers of old-fashioned clothes amazingly quickly. Dulcie, in the next cubicle, kindly helped her with the endless buttons. Flora hurried into the horrible but comfy blue pyjamas she found under her pillow.

The bed was strange – sheets and blankets instead of

a duvet — but Flora's darling old bear from home was sitting on the pillow, with his bald nose and — wait a moment, this was not her bear. He belonged to the other Flora. Her own bear was at Penrice Hall. But this one somehow felt very friendly and familiar.

"Your bear's nice," said Dulcie.

Flora looked at her sharply, to check she was not having a laugh — none of her friends talked about childish soft toys. But Dulcie was innocently cuddling a large, floppy white rabbit. "This is Mr Bunny. I've had him since I was a baby."

The bell rang again. The girls switched off the lamps beside their beds. The room sank into mysterious shadow. After a few moments, Flora's eyes adjusted. The curtains were not drawn, and the night was clear. She could soon see the shapes of the others quite clearly, and the bright glitter of their eyes in the shadows.

"We have to keep quiet for ten minutes," Pete whispered. "Until Harbottle goes off to listen to the news, then we can talk."

"Who's Harbottle?"

"Shhh! She's an old barnacle, but we can't talk yet!"

The ten minutes seemed to last for ages. Eventually, a door was heard to close along the corridor. Then the questions began again, this time in loud whispers.

Pogo asked, "Do you all have your own private aeroplanes in the future?"

47

"No, of course not," said Flora. "Not unless you're a rock star."

"Golly, what's that?"

"If you're from the future," Dulcie said, "shouldn't you be wearing a silver suit?"

Pete snorted with laughter. "Don't be such a chump – she's from Wimbledon, not Mars!"

Flora was a little insulted by the cheerful way Pete was taking this, as if being pulled back through time was a joke. "Would someone please tell me how I got here?"

"We cast a spell," said Dulcie.

"You what?"

"You're telling it wrong!" Pete's voice rose alarmingly.

"Shhh!" hissed Dulcie and Pogo.

"All right, but let me tell. It started last term, when we decided to explore the attics."

"Not that we're allowed up there," Pogo put in. "But Ethel sleeps up there, and she told us she'd heard queer noises through the wall. We were hunting for ghosts."

"Please, Pogo!" snapped Pete. "Didn't you hear me say I was doing the telling?" (Pete was in charge here, Flora noted, or thought she was.) "That's when we discovered the secret room. We were staggered nobody had ever noticed it before. In fact, it was Pogo who worked it out first."

"Yes, I'm the intellectual in this bedroom," said Pogo.

"I remembered that there were eight windows on the attic floor – we went outside and counted them, just to be sure – but we only found seven doors. The eighth door, next to Ethel's, had been covered up and papered over. Naturally, we were all wild to know what was going on."

"I was scared," Dulcie whispered. "I thought there might be dead bodies up there. Or mice."

"Look, belt up, you two – let me finish, or we'll be here all night." Pete turned back to Flora. "We got into the secret room by climbing out of Ethel's window and crawling along the gutter."

"Not as crazy as it sounds," put in Pogo. "The gutter's more like a small balcony with a stone rail – even Dulcie managed it."

"Oh, don't – it was so awful!"

"Anyway," Pete went on, "we got the window open, and it was pretty easy to climb into the hidden room – though everything was absolutely covered in dust. The room was empty, except for three big trunks. They weren't locked, so we opened them. The first was full of books – really old books. The second was just papers and writing, and the third was just sort of chemistry stuff – glass tubes and things."

"The books were full of odd pictures," Dulcie said. "Birds with men's heads, funny little diagrams of suns and moons—"

"Most of them had queer writing we couldn't understand," said Pogo. "But one was in English, and we took it away with us – I'll show you." She jumped out of her bed and went over to the rug beside the window. She pulled this back and lifted up one of the floorboards underneath. "This is our secret hiding place, by the way. You mustn't tell anyone about it." She took something out and brought it over to Flora.

It was too dark to see more than an ancient, mouldy-smelling book with rough, floppy pages. In the dim light, Flora made out pictures of people in weird clothes. The writing on the first page was so large and black that she could read it: "An Olde Wife's Compendium of Remedies, Spells and Enchantements".

"It's such a scream," Pete said. "There's a cure for lovesickness, there's a spell for making bread rise, and there're heaps of spells for making rain or sunshine – not that any of them worked when we tried them – mainly because they all seemed to need things like snail's horns and cobwebs gathered at dawn." She grinned wickedly. "We even cast a spell to make our worst enemy go bald but, unfortunately, her golden locks remained firmly attached to her evil head. Such a disappointment."

"And we tried turning the lead from our pencils into gold," said Pogo. "That didn't work either. You're our first success."

Flora frowned. "Success" was the wrong word for a disaster like this. "I still don't understand – why did you bring me here?"

"It was called a 'Summoning'," Pete said. "There's a whole chapter of them. We chose a spell that would ensure the blessing of a happy life by summoning a helpful demon from the future – I must say, you're not my idea of a demon. I'm glad you don't have horns and a pitchfork."

"It obviously doesn't mean the horrid sort of demon," Dulcie said quickly. "This demon is supposed to know all the bad things that are going to happen to you – like being struck by lightning, or run over by a tram – and stop them happening."

"I don't want to be rude," said Pogo, "but I don't think you're what we ordered – unless you've come to warn us about lightning, or something."

"Of course not!" Flora hissed furiously. "I've no idea what's going to happen to any of you – and I don't bloody care!"

The others were shocked. Dulcie gasped.

"Don't you see what you've done to me?" Flora was shaking with anger. "You fooled about with old spells – and thanks to you, my life's ruined! Send me back right now!"

The three girls exchanged looks of dismay.

"What's stopping you? I have to get back to my own

time. Do the reversing spell, or whatever it is – light the candles and put the sheets on your head – and I don't care if you all get bloody ponies, or whatever you call them."

All three girls gasped aloud at this. Pete's eyes had a gleam of fascination.

"The thing is," Pogo said slowly, "there isn't exactly a reversing spell. We – well, we're frightfully sorry, and all that – but we haven't the faintest idea how to send you back."

"But you must!" Flora cried. "Or I'm stuck here in the past!" The terrible sense of loneliness swept over her again, as it had done in the head's study. She didn't cry this time. She felt cold and afraid. "Don't you see what this means? I'll have to stay here and grow up with someone else's parents – my own parents haven't even been born yet. Thanks to you and your stupid magic, I've lost my friends, my home – everything!"

The three girls were silent for a long time. They were starting to understand the seriousness of what they had done.

"We never dreamed it would work," Pete said.

"We didn't think the demon would be a real girl," Dulcie whispered.

"I'm your responsibility now," Flora said. "You brought me here, so you'd better find out how to get me back."

"But how?" Dulcie asked.

"That's your problem. Right now, you all have to help me as much as possible."

"Of course we will!" said Pete.

"I'm not doing any homework," Flora snapped – why were they all taking it so lightly? "I was on my way to a modern school where they don't have any homework."

"Crikey, I've heard about schools like that," said Pete. "Are your people vegetarians?"

"And there are swimming pools, and you can order takeaways . . ." Flora sighed, thinking of Penrice Hall, which now seemed like Paradise. "And you call the teachers by their first names."

Dulcie giggled. "You're telling stories!"

"We'd have to call Bradley 'Mavis'," said Pete.

Pete, Pogo and Dulcie burst into an explosion of giggles.

"I'm not doing any kind of work while I'm here." Flora was impatient. What was there to laugh about? Didn't they get that they'd ruined her life? "And I expect you lot to work twenty-four/seven till you find out how to send me home."

The three girls were silent for a moment.

Pete said, "I'm sorry, Flora. This whole thing is mostly my fault – it was all my idea. I'll do everything I can to help you."

"Me, too," whispered Dulcie.

"And me, and I'll start by giving you a word of warning," Pogo said, in her posh, dry little voice. "If you don't want to get in the most awful trouble, watch your language."

"Oh, Pogo – honestly!" Pete tossed her head scornfully. "You're such a Victorian!"

"No, I'm not. I'm stating the facts. Words like – like the ones you said just now will probably get you expelled – and that would make things even worse."

Pete's eyes gleamed at Flora through the dim light. "You're right, that would be a catastrophe. You'd better listen to her, Flora – Rhoda Pugh heard me say 'damn' last term, and she was so boiling mad she gave me two ponies."

Flora did not want to be expelled. She didn't like this awful place – but if she was expelled and sent back to India, that wretched spell would never be reversed. "OK, I'll do my best not to say anything rude – but you might have to tell me." She wriggled into her strange bed, with its smooth, slippery sheets, and absently picked up the bear. "Damn isn't such a big deal where I come from."

Where did she come from? When she thought of home, she saw her bedroom in Wimbledon – but she also saw a hot room with wooden blinds, where the bed was shrouded in white nets. This must be the room of the other Flora, who had come from British India in

1935, and was now (lucky cow) revelling in the luxuries of Penrice Hall.

From the next bed, Dulcie whispered, "Goodnight, Flora!"

"Goodnight." And Flora fell into an oddly delicious deep sleep.

6

The Carver

"Wake up! Flora, wake up! Breakfast's in twenty minutes!" A bell was clanging, and someone was shaking her shoulder. Flora groaned. She knew, before she opened her eyes, that she was still trapped in 1935.

When she did open them, the first thing she saw was the rosy face of Dulcie. "Hello. Are you still – you know – from the future?"

"Yes," Flora said crossly. "You'd better start keeping your promise." She rolled out of bed and put on the other Flora's scratchy wool dressing gown and slippers. "What's up with Pete?"

"Miss Peterson doesn't like mornings," Pogo said, grinning. "Take no notice."

Pete sat slumped on the edge of her bed, her eyes invisible behind a mess of untidy hair. She looked as if she had spent the night in a wind tunnel.

Flora wished Granny could see this. According to Granny, young girls in the past leapt eagerly out of bed at dawn and immediately jumped into an ice-cold bath. Pete had to be dragged off the bed by Pogo, and helped into her dressing gown like a sleepwalker.

"Come on," Dulcie said kindly, slipping her warm hand into Flora's. "I'll show you what to do."

Flora's head was soon swimming with the strangeness of it all. Her first day at APS last September had been stressful enough (especially with Ella suddenly not being her best friend any more), but at least she hadn't had to learn the customs of an ancient civilization.

First, there was the horror of the cloakroom. It was freezing cold and smelled of disinfectant. The doors of the toilet cubicles did not lock, and you had to sit there holding the door with one hand, to stop other girls blundering in. You had to queue for the sinks – and when Flora got to the front of the queue, a tall girl with bright yellow hair roughly shoved her aside.

"Hey!" Flora protested. "I'm next!"

"Not any more, maggot!"

"But I was before you!" Why weren't the others doing anything to help? Furiously, Flora tried to elbow the horrible girl out of the way.

Pogo quickly grabbed her arm. "Pax – pax! She's new, and she's really sorry!" She hustled Flora to the sink at the end of the row, muttering, "Don't fight with her!"

"But she's a cow!"

"Shhh! Just hurry up!"

Flora wanted to argue, but there wasn't time to do more than brush her teeth (the 1930s toothpaste tasted of chalk), splash her face with water and drag a comb through her stupid new hairstyle.

"Why didn't you stick up for me?" she demanded, when they were back in the bedroom. "You must've seen her pushing me!"

Pogo briskly pulled her gymslip (which was what they called the boxy black pinafores) over her head. "We ought to have warned you – that's Consuela Carver."

"The one we tried to make bald," Dulcie added.

"Yes, and if she'd heard you calling her a cow, she'd have got you into no end of trouble."

"What could she do to me?"

"She says such mean things," said Dulcie, trying to dress herself and help Flora at the same time. "And she finds ways to spoil your work."

"Why don't you just tell one of the teachers?"

Dulcie was shocked. "You can't do that!"

"Why not?"

"Because," Pogo said firmly, "they'll think you're a beastly sneak."

"A sneak?"

"You know – a telltale."

Flora was impatient. "So you just let that cow push you around? Oh, all right! I won't use that word. But what's her problem, anyway?"

"Me," said Pete, scrabbling at the buttons on her inky white blouse. "I accidentally whacked her on the bottom with my hockey stick last term, and she wouldn't believe it was an accident – oh, BLOW! My top button's come off!"

Pogo said, "In this bedroom, we've made a vow of 'All for one and one for all!' – like the Three Musketeers. If the Carver is Pete's foe, she's our foe. Now that you're one of us, you must avoid the Carver as much as possible. Also her guards and toadies – Mary Denby, Gladys Pyecroft, Wendy Elliot—"

"This is ridiculous!" snapped Flora. "If the teachers refuse to do anything about the dreadful bullying problem here, you should complain to your parents!"

For some reason, the others seemed to think this was silly.

"Crikey, no!" said Pogo. "I'd only get a lecture about standing up for myself."

"So would I," Pete said, looking at Flora rather scornfully. "And I'd jolly well deserve it – imagine writing to your people to tell them you're a coward!"

"Pete, come on," Pogo said. "There isn't time to fiddle with your button – just hoist up your tie – we don't want to start Flora off with a pony for being late!"

Pogo was a sensible little thing, Flora thought; far sharper than Pete, though Pete was convinced she was the leader in this bedroom. It was Pogo who led them all down to breakfast. They joined the crowd of girls in identical black gymslips, trooping along the corridor and down the big staircase – all spookily quiet, except for a few sleepy whispers.

What time was it, anyway? Practically dawn. Flora had a second of intense longing for the mornings she had at home, in the twenty-first century. She could almost smell her passion-flower shower gel, and Dad's coffee, and almond croissants warmed in the microwave. There was a smell of food here, but it was like boiled blankets.

"I nearly forgot," Pogo muttered, "breakfast is in French."

"It's – what?"

"Shh! We're supposed to keep quiet till after Peepy's said the prayer. And then we have to speak in French."

"Why?"

"Never mind why!" They were approaching the dining hall, and Pogo lowered her voice. "It's simply one of the rules."

"Well, it's a silly rule," Flora said. "What's the point, when we all speak perfectly good English?"

"Shhhh!" hissed Pogo and Dulcie.

As they entered the dining room, all the girls became eerily silent – Flora had never known an entire school could be this quiet. It wasn't natural. And making them speak French – that was child abuse.

The hall was big and draughty, like a church. Hundreds of girls stood in silent lines at the four long tables. The breakfast now smelled of wet socks. At one end of the hall was a raised table, where the teachers stood, also in silence. The headmistress stomped royally to the centre of the top table. She said something that Flora thought might be Latin. Everyone murmured, "Amen." Then Miss Powers-Prout said something that sounded like, "*Bonjour memzel, assayer voo*." There was an explosion of chairs scraping as everyone sat down.

A bit of talking broke out round the table, but Flora, despite several years of French lessons and two holidays in France, couldn't remember a word of French, except, "*Coca-Cola, s'il vous plaît*" (and "*Pas devant les enfants*", which was what Dad said to Granny when she started on about her husbands). She looked down at her breakfast. There was a pale, scummy cup of tea, a slice of white bread and butter and a bowl of slimy porridge.

"Yuck," she said, "what a carb-fest! Don't they know anything about healthy eating? At home I have mangoes and nectarines, and sometimes a croissant—" She broke off. The whole table had gone quiet, and they were all staring at her. Consuela Carver sat opposite. She giggled nastily. Flora's face burned.

"Flora," Virginia Denning said, from the end of the table, *"eel fo parlay fransay."*

"Elle ay tray stoopeed, nez par?" sneered the yellow-haired girl.

Flora understood "stoopeed". She decided she hated the Carver, and she absolutely knew it after breakfast, when everyone was surging out into the hall, and the cow brushed past her, saying loudly, "At home I have mangoes and nectarines – and a nice hot curry!"

"Beast!" muttered Pete. "Take no notice."

Flora was still stinging from the "stoopeed" crack. "You three are supposed to be looking after me," she snapped. "So you'd better keep her out of my way."

The three girls looked at each other uneasily.

Pogo said, "That might be tricky."

"I don't care how tricky it is! Let me remind you, I didn't ask to come here, and I refuse to spend my time being bullied by someone from the past who isn't even real!"

"Of course this is real!" cried Pete. "You're the one who's not real!"

"I am real! I belong in the twenty-first century and you three are just – just – shadows!"

"Shadows?" Pete scowled. Her gaze locked with Flora's, and the two girls glared at each other. Pete was revving up for an argument. "You're the shadowy one – when you appeared at the summoning, we could see right through you!"

Flora was annoyed. "I'm sorry if you don't like it, but the fact is that everything that happens to you has happened already – what you think of as 'now' is really 'then' – so you are sort of shadows, aren't you?"

"This is a shadow, is it?" Pete pinched Flora's arm.

"Ow!" Flora gasped. "That really hurt!"

"So I'm real after all, am I?"

"Don't!" Dulcie blurted out.

"Stow it, Pete," Pogo said quietly. "You can't fight with Flora. We got her into this mess, and we're honour-bound to get her out of it. That's all there is to it."

Pete lifted her head proudly and pressed her lips together. After a short silence, she muttered, "Sorry."

She was not sorry. Flora rubbed her arm angrily. Her chest felt tight, and she was afraid she might cry. Pete could be horrible. Why didn't Dulcie and Pogo stand up to her more?

Dulcie took her hand again. "We have to go back upstairs now. We have fifteen minutes to make our beds and then it's assembly. Come on."

Despite having all these servants, the school expected them to make their own beds. This wasn't easy, with all the sheets and blankets, and the slippery "eiderdown" that looked like a duvet but wasn't. Flora could not make it all look tidy. She gave up halfway through, and waited for Dulcie and Pogo to finish the job. Pete did not lift a finger to help – but she was struggling with her own bed, which was like a heap of washing. In the end, Dulcie and Pogo did all the work.

After this, Flora was taken down to assembly, which happened in a huge room across the hall from the place where they had breakfast. The entire school filed in silently, and sat in rows of hard chairs. Old Peepy read something from the Bible, and made an announcement about a nature ramble the following week. They sang a hymn called "Come Down, O Love Divine". A thin lady with clip-on glasses played the piano.

It was quieter and more boring than assemblies at APS. Otherwise, it wasn't too dramatically different, and Flora felt a little calmer. She was sorry now that she had fought with Pete. For some reason, she wanted this awful, headstrong girl to like her.

It was partly my fault, she thought. *I didn't have to call her a shadow.*

Before she had a chance to patch things up with Pete, however, Virginia Denning came up to them.

"Morning, maggot."

A crowd of girls – now chattering just as loudly as any girls at a modern school – milled around in the hall, under the forbidding portrait of Dame Mildred Beak.

Flora said, "Hi, Virginia – I mean, hello."

The older girl's green eyes were friendly. "I hope you're settling in."

"Yes, thanks."

"Someone should've warned you about the French."

"We did," Pogo said.

"She didn't listen," said Pete.

"Hmmm, well, never mind. I've come to march you off to matron – you three can scoot."

"But . . ." Flora began. She looked helplessly at Dulcie, Pogo and Pete. She hadn't expected to be left alone, and she wasn't sure she could cope.

Dulcie quickly patted her arm. "Don't worry. Matron's a darling."

"Pete," Virginia said, "your tie is at half-mast. Has someone died?"

"I've lost the top button of my blouse. And my collar keeps coming open and the knot keeps slipping."

"You'd better sew the button back at first break, or Harbottle will have the vapours. Come along, Flora."

Reluctantly, Flora followed her, feeling small and nervous without her three guardians. Virginia handed her over to a short, round woman with a puff of grey hair under a starched white cap. Matron had a strong Scottish accent. She wore a very stiff white apron, and had gold-rimmed glasses on a long chain. Her room smelled exactly like the medical room at APS.

Flora wondered if there was any way a trained nurse could spot that she was from the future. All Matron said, however, was that Flora was "a wee bit thin".

"Thanks," Flora said.

Matron did not hear this. "Never mind. We'll soon fatten you up."

She made Flora take a spoonful of "tonic" that tasted disgusting. Flora did not want to be "fattened". Wasn't it good to be thin? How ghastly if this stuff worked, and she was fat when she got back to her own time.

The horrid taste of the tonic lingered in her mouth as she followed Matron back to the bedroom to unpack her boxes – or rather, the other Flora's boxes. This was interesting. Once you got past the piles of vests and knickers, the other Flora owned some nice things. She liked the heavy fountain pen, and the writing case made of soft red leather. She also liked the small, rolled-up leather case full of needles and threads and stuff for sewing. Matron said it was called a "hussif".

"And a very good one it is, too," she said approvingly. "You'll be mending your own clothes while you're here." She pointed to a hole that had somehow appeared in Flora's stocking. "You can start with this – I expect you to show me a beautiful darn."

Flora made a mental note to ask the others what a "darn" was.

"Now, put your writing things in your satchel."

The satchel was made of brown leather. This was how she would carry her stuff around the school – like the backpack she took to APS.

When the unpacking was finished, Matron took Flora to her form room. "In you go, dear." And she trotted away.

Flora took several deep breaths and pushed open the door.

Twenty heads turned round. Twenty pairs of eyes stared at her. Her head swam. She searched for her three friends, and the first face she made out belonged to horrible, sneering Consuela Carver. Like many class cows, the Carver was the first person you saw because she was – in an evil sort of way – very pretty, with her bright golden curls and big blue eyes. The expression in those eyes made Flora feel slightly sick.

Miss Bradley – with a black gown over her tweed suit – was at the front of the class. "Ah, the new girl – come here, dear."

It wasn't a big room, but the walk up to Miss Bradley seemed to take ages.

"Girls, this is Flora Fox. She's come all the way from

India, and I hope you'll do your best to make her feel welcome. Yours is the desk next to Dulcie's."

It was comforting to see Dulcie's kind pink face. Flora sat down at the vacant desk beside her. It was the old-fashioned sort of school desk with a sloping lid. It had a few spots of ink, but nobody had written anything on it. At APS she shared a table with Yasmin, Jessica and Kylie.

On the veranda at home, there was an old card table with a green baize top, and Fritz the monkey perched on the top step, chattering to himself and daintily eating a banana. They had to stop lessons when the sun was too hot and the sweat dripped off the ends of their pigtails.

If only the other Flora would leave her alone – fighting off her memories was exhausting. It took all her effort, and she couldn't think straight.

"You catch us in the middle of our history lesson," Miss Bradley said. "We're learning about the campaigns of the Duke of Marlborough". On the blackboard behind her was written: "Blenheim – Ramillies – Oudenarde – Malplaquet". It was all gobbledegook to Flora. Blackboards were yet another weird thing. When Miss Bradley wrote something, the chalk squeaked unpleasantly, and when she banged the felt board-rubber it puffed out white clouds of dust.

Miss Bradley caught her bewilderment. "Don't worry, it's all in the book. You can read the chapter for your prep tonight. What were you studying at home?"

"The Saxons," Flora said. "And something about the Corn Laws."

There were scattered giggles. Miss Bradley's lips twitched, as if she were trying not to smile. "Something? That they were repealed, for instance?"

"I – I don't know." The heat rushed back into Flora's face. The Corn Laws had come from the memories of the other Flora. She made an effort to remember her last history lesson with Ms Stuart at APS. "We made a Saxon castle, out of cardboard."

More giggles. It was so frustrating – they all thought she was completely thick, and didn't realize her brain was split between two centuries.

"And – and we were going to do a project about the Second World War."

After a second of astonished silence, the whole class erupted into shrieks of laughter. Consuela Carver was in absolute hysterics, and so were Pete and Dulcie and Miss Bradley.

The only person not laughing was Pogo, who was staring at her with a mixture of fascination and alarm. Flora suddenly remembered that the Second World War hadn't happened yet. It wasn't due to start for another four years – she was pretty sure it started in 1939, because they had a mug at home with the dates on.

This was so embarrassing. She wanted to disappear. Everything she knew was jumbled up with everything the other Flora knew, until she didn't know which was which. And the frightening thing was that when she tried to concentrate on the future, she felt her memories of the twenty-first century rolling about chaotically, like beads from a broken necklace.

"All right, simmer down, everyone!" Miss Bradley was still chuckling. "I'm glad to say there has been only one world war, Flora, and nobody's in a hurry to repeat the experience!"

The laughing stopped, and Miss Bradley began to talk about battles. She wrote some dates on the blackboard. Flora wrote them down in the notebook she had found in her satchel, because this was what everyone else was doing, but she was thinking about what she had blurted out just now. There was a big difference between knowing a war had happened in the past and knowing one was about to happen in the future. If she did not get home to the future, she would see it.

7

Harbottle

After history with Miss Bradley it was geography with Miss Horton. Pogo helped Flora to gather up her books and put them in her satchel. She led her out of the classroom into the corridor.

"I can't wait to ask you about this war," she muttered into Flora's ear. "But we'd better wait till we're alone – unless you want the whole school knowing you're from the future. You'd better try not to blurt out anything else."

"I was mixed up, that's all," Flora hissed crossly. "Something weird's happened to my brain – thanks to you lot and your stupid spell."

"What do you mean?"

She couldn't explain, and this made her crosser. "I

don't know – it's like there's stuff I'm not allowed to remember about the future – when I try, I just get a lot of old Indian memories from the other Flora."

"Well, do your best not to make any more staggering statements before lunch."

"Of course I won't!"

Geography, fortunately, was less bewildering than history had been – perhaps her brain was starting to settle down. The lesson was quite easy to understand. Miss Horton had chalked a map of Europe on the blackboard, and the girls had to write in the names of the rivers and cities. This time, Flora's memory did not let her down. She remembered some things from APS and some things from the map of the world in the Wimbledon kitchen, and Miss Horton said she had been "well grounded".

Lunch was disgusting, but she was so hungry that she ate every scrap of the pale meat, boiled potatoes and soggy boiled cabbage. For pudding there was a lump of stodgy cake, topped with red jam and custard. It was surprisingly delicious, and Flora had a second helping.

At APS you lined up with a tray to get things like filled rolls, chips and drinks in cartons. At St Winifred's, the food was dolloped out by a squad of servants. One of them was Ethel, and she gave Flora a very friendly smile. Flora smiled back, to show she was grateful to Ethel for unpacking her bag last night.

On the other side of the table, Pete took a small silver coin out of the leg of her knickers, and put it on the table. Ethel quickly picked it up while she served Pete's pudding.

"She buys us sweets," Dulcie explained (luckily, lunch was in English). "We're not allowed to go down to the village until the fourth form."

"It's enormously secret," Pogo said, on Flora's other side. "Don't tell anyone, or we'll all be in hot water."

Flora pushed away her bowl. "How can you think about sweets? I've never been so full!"

"Oh, you wait," Dulcie said. "You'll be ravenous again by teatime."

"We ought to think about this afternoon." Pogo frowned. She glanced across the table at Pete, who was busily talking to the red-haired girl next to her, and taking no notice of her friends.

Pete's already tired of me, Flora thought bitterly. *She resents having to look after me.*

Pete was a selfish, lazy person who only did nice things when it didn't cost her any effort. The whole stupid summoning spell had been her idea, but she left all the hard slog to Pogo and Dulcie.

Pogo spoke in a low voice. "I'm afraid it's Latin with Miss Harbottle, and she's a gorgon. You'd better keep as quiet as possible and pray she doesn't notice you. She's very mean, and so incredibly old that she probably taught Florence Nightingale – you do know who Florence Nightingale was, don't you?"

"Yes," Flora said. "The nurse. She's still famous in my century."

"Well, keep your head down – this is no time to give yourself away."

"Don't worry. I'll be careful." Flora didn't really see what the fuss was about. The woman was only a teacher. How bad could it be?

The classroom door opened with a crash. It was like a cold wind rushing in. Every girl sprang to her feet.

Miss Harbottle was tiny – hardly taller than Flora – dressed in a black teacher's gown very rusty at the seams. Her lips were thin, her eyes were little and beady, and she looked like an angry, wrinkled turtle.

She faced the class. "*Salvete.*"

Everyone chorused "*Salve!*" and sat down.

"Good afternoon, gels." Her voice was deep and gravelly. "It is our first lesson this term, so let us pick up where we left orf. Daphne Peterson."

Pete stood up. "Yes, Miss Harbottle."

"Remind us – what did we talk about in our last lesson, all those weeks ago?"

"I – I—" Pete's face turned bright red (*now she knows how it feels*, Flora thought meanly). "Was it – one of Pliny's letters?"

"I should think it was, since we spent the whole of last term studying the younger Pliny's letters. And what was he writing about?"

Pete held up her head proudly, as if facing a firing squad. "I don't remember."

"You – are – an – IMBECILE," croaked the turtle-mouth. "And a HALFWIT – and a NINNY! You are also a SLATTERN – where is your collar button? You will report to me tomorrow morning before breakfast, and if I find ONE HAIR out of place, you will earn yourself a *poena*."

"Yes, Miss Harbottle."

"Sit DOWN."

Pete collapsed thankfully into her chair.

"Consuela Carver."

"Yes, Miss Harbottle." The Carver stood up.

"Please refresh Daphne's memory."

Smoothly, the Carver said, "The letter was about a man who was murdered in his bath by his slaves."

"Thank you. Sit down."

Consuela Carver sat down, unbearably smug.

"New gel."

Flora slid a quick glance at Pete, still red-faced and miserable, and stopped feeling mean.

"NEW GEL!"

Fart and bum, Harbottle was talking to her. Flora leapt to her feet. "Yes, Miss Harbottle."

"Are you DEAF?"

"N-no, Miss Harbottle."

"In that case, you are a DAYDREAMER, and I do not tolerate daydreamers in any class of mine. Let us wake you up with a little mental exercise. Open the book at page sixty-five, and translate the first paragraph."

Flora looked down at the dark red book Dulcie had placed on her desk before the lesson. It was called *A Shorter Latin Primer*.

"I'm waiting," said Miss Harbottle.

She was horrible, with her grating voice and spiteful little eyes – as if she wanted you to fail. Flora felt her face turning hot.

"I can't do it," she said. "And before you call me names, it's not my fault. I've never had a Latin lesson in my life."

A shudder of horror passed through the silent girls.

"Really? Your father informs us that you have been learning Latin for three years – am I to take it that he is a LIAR?"

"No—" (Bum!)

"NO? Then YOU must be the liar – logically, only one of you can be telling the truth. Page sixty-five, if you please."

Flora opened the book and found the page, with shaking hands. Why did it look familiar?

It was past eleven, and the sun climbed relentlessly.

Drowsy in the heat, Flora did her best to concentrate while Miss Foster took them through the translation for the umpteenth time, mainly for the benefit of Joan from next door, who was a year older but rather dim.

"*Balbus has built a wall. The wall is well made, and pleases him. Drusilla is the wife of Balbus. The well-made wall pleases Drusilla.*"

"So you HAVE learned Latin!" croaked Harbottle.

Flora realized she had read it out loud. For once, the memories of the other Flora had come in useful. "I don't know—"

"And now she DOESN'T KNOW!"

"What I mean is, I don't know how I know."

"Let me tell you, Flora Fox, that I do not tolerate such UNDERHAND behaviour. For your prep tonight, you will write out all the verbs on page twenty-six."

"Yes, Miss Harbottle," Flora said miserably.

"If this is the kind of gel they're sending from the colonies these days," Harbottle said, "I DESPAIR. Stand up straight when I'm talking to you!"

There was a burst of giggling, hastily stifled.

"I have seldom heard anything as appalling as your accent, never mind your grammar – are you a lady or a kitchenmaid? Sit DOWN, and pay ATTENTION!"

Flora sat down, trembling. This old woman was a witch. She thought of her warm, noisy classroom at APS, and had to swallow several times, so she didn't cry.

St Winifred's was a bad dream. The others had to find the reversing spell, before she died of unhappiness.

After the Latin lesson, things were a little better. The lessons were baffling, but the teachers were nicer. They had tea, and Flora discovered that she owned a tuck box. The parents of the other Flora had been generous. The large wooden box, which she found in her cubbyhole in the box room, was packed with jam, chocolate, honey and a sticky fruit cake in a tin. It was supposed to last until the end of term. Flora allowed herself a small bar of chocolate, in an antique Cadbury's wrapper, and took a jar of strawberry jam to spread on her teatime bread and butter.

After tea, the girls did homework – "prep", as they called it – in the lower-school common room. This was a large, shabby, comfortable room, furnished with tables and big, sagging armchairs. Flora had no intention of doing any homework. She handed hers over to Pete, who looked furious.

"Why do I have to do your blasted Latin verbs?"

"Keep your voice down," Pogo said. "You know perfectly well why. Now, stop complaining – the Latin's by far the easiest. Unless you'd rather do her maths."

"Why can't Dulcie do it?"

Pogo was stern. "You know how slow she is – no offence, Dulcie, but you do take ages."

"You're quite right," Dulcie said mildly. "Granny says I'm constitutionally incapable of hurrying. I live with my grandmother," she added to Flora, "just like you – I mean, when you go home to the future."

"Poor you," Flora said – though she wouldn't have minded Granny if she could see Mum and Dad. Thinking about Mum and Dad brought out all kinds of worries. Were they all right? Had they noticed that the girl they spoke to at Penrice Hall wasn't their real daughter?

Dulcie said, "Oh, my granny's not like yours. She's a darling – and she's only had one husband. I've always lived with her, because my parents are dead."

"Oh . . ." Flora was shocked, and very sorry for Dulcie. "How sh— I mean, how awful."

"They both died when I was a baby," Dulcie said. "It's all right. I don't remember them, so I don't really miss them."

"Judging by the contents of your tuck box," Pogo said, "I'd guess your granny is the spoiling sort. I've never seen so much fudge."

Dulcie smiled. "Yes, she spoils me terribly. She says she has to love me for three."

"She'd better go easy," said Pete, "or you'll be the size of three!"

Flora thought this was mean, but it made Dulcie giggle delightedly.

Pogo, Pete and Dulcie found space at one of the tables and settled down to their homework – and Flora's. Of course they were all annoyed about this, though Pete was the only one who showed it. Flora went to the other side of the room and curled up in a vacant armchair. She had the other Flora's lovely red writing case on her knee, and it was sad that she had nobody to write to.

How great it would be if she could write a letter to Ella. Even if they had not been in different centuries, however, Ella was no longer her best friend. Yasmin was easier to boss than Ella, but she didn't understand things in the same way.

Flora opened the writing case. On the sheet of blotting paper, someone had pencilled, "Write to us often, darling!"

Flora had stared and stared, until the hanky her mother waved was no bigger than a white speck. They had both tried hard to be brave, but when Flora stood on the dock at Southampton and Mother waved from the boat, they were both crying.

For the first time, Flora felt sorry for the other Flora. Yesterday she had felt too sorry for herself to care about the girl who had taken her place. She had only envied her for having television and proper bathrooms at the luxurious Penrice Hall. Now, she saw how bewildering it must be to land in the next century –

and how lonely.

Other Flora, I wonder what you're doing now, at this very moment across time? Perhaps you're thinking about your mother, and waving goodbye to her on the boat. Perhaps you're thinking about my mother, and how she looked when I was pulling away on the train. I wish I could talk to you.

The room was quiet, except for scattered murmurs and the sound of pens scratching on paper. Flora went to the bookcase beside one of the long windows. At home in the future, she didn't much like reading. She had never really understood how Ella could like books more than films – her ex-best friend always had her nose in a book. In 1935, however, there was nothing else to do except read. These books had hard covers in drab colours, and Flora didn't recognize any of the titles, except *The Secret Garden*, a "classic" Mum had given her last Christmas.

She took this back to the big, sagging, comfortable armchair, beside the scorching gas fire, and started to read. The story was surprisingly gripping – it opened in British India, where the other Flora came from, and both the heroine's parents died of fever in the first chapter.

Flora was almost sorry when Dulcie came up to her to tell her prep was over.

"We have a free hour before bedtime," she explained.

"It's for practising music or going to clubs. Or we can just go up to our bedrooms."

"Let's go to the bedroom," Flora said, closing her book. "I'm so tired of pretending not to be modern. And someone has to mend my stocking."

The three girls looked at each other, and Pete rolled her eyes rudely.

"I'll do it," Dulcie said.

"But I wanted you to do my collar button!" cried Pete. "That's not fair!"

"You could try doing it yourself," suggested Pogo.

"Oh, very funny – you know I'll make a complete bish of it! Now I'll get another pony – and it's all Flora's fault!"

"Crap!" Flora gasped, too angry at the injustice to care about minding her language. "This is your fault! You made me come here!"

"Yes, and I can't wait to send you back!"

Pogo put her hand on Pete's arm. "Steady on, old thing."

"Oh, all right. Sorry." Pete didn't look sorry. She looked like thunder. When they reached their bedroom, she flung herself on her bed with a dramatic moan. "What an utterly putrid day! I had no idea it'd be such beastly hard labour! It's like dragging round a ball and chain!"

This was very insulting. Tears rushed to Flora's eyes.

82

"You – you mustn't be horrid to Flora," Dulcie said, pink with determination. "She can't help it."

"You only like her because she's as gormless as you are."

Dulcie's soft lower lip quivered. Her innocent eyes filled with tears.

"That's enough, Pete," Pogo said angrily. "If you're mean to Dulcie, I'll jolly well punch you – and hang the pony!"

Pete scowled round at them all. Flora guessed that she was already ashamed of being mean to Dulcie. "Look, I'm sorry – all right? But you must admit how frightful this is – extra homework, extra sewing – when she's not asking stupid questions, she's complaining!"

"It just won't do, that's all," Pogo said, folding her arms decisively. "You can huff and puff all you like – but Flora's still our responsibility, and we gave her our word!"

Pete was cross and uncomfortable, and would not look properly at Flora. "I'm beginning to wonder if she is from the future, anyway – I think she's just playing tricks on us!"

There was a silence. Pogo looked very thoughtfully at Flora. Her eyes were small and pale, and as shrewd as the bright little eyes of Fritz the monkey in the other Flora's memories.

"I believe her," she said. "I can't put my finger on it. There's something about her that's just – different."

"What about that rubbish about a Second World War?"

"Oh, yes," Pogo said, turning to Flora. "Now you can tell us about this war."

"She made it up," snapped Pete.

"I did not!" snapped Flora.

"Who's the enemy going to be?" Pogo asked.

"Perhaps it's invaders from another planet!" sneered Pete.

Flora muttered, "Don't be so stupid – it's the Germans."

"Is that the best you can do? Why on earth would we fight the Germans again?"

"The Germans have only just got back on their feet after the Great War," Pogo said. "The last thing their chancellor wants is another one." She frowned. "Still, I'll write to my brother Neville, and see what he thinks. He's at Cambridge, and he's frightfully interested in politics."

"Don't tell me you believe her!" shouted Pete.

"Well, if I believe she's from the future," Pogo said reasonably, "I have to believe she's telling the truth about the war. And I do believe it. You can see she's not the sort to make up something like this. We should be taking advantage of the situation."

"How? What advantage?"

Pogo turned back to Flora. "I'm not exactly sure, but we should be finding out everything we can about what's going to happen to us all."

Flora sighed. Pogo's curiosity was almost as awkward as Pete's refusal to believe her. "I'll do my best, but as I keep telling you, my memories are all over the place. I know the Second World War started − starts − in 1939, and I'm pretty sure Britain won, but that's about it. And I haven't a clue what's going to happen to you lot."

Pete looked at her coldly. "Well, you're a fat lot of use. There'd be some point to you if you knew the names of all the horses that are going to win the Derby, so we could bet all our pocket money and get rich. But all you do is drivel on about things that won't be invented till we're old − what's the point of that?"

"The thing is," Dulcie said, "we sort of invited Flora, didn't we? And when you've invited someone, you can't just ignore them, can you? That would be frightfully rude."

Flora suddenly remembered how she had begged Ella to come to Italy last summer. When they were there, she had been irritated because Ella seemed to expect so much attention.

I was rather lazy about looking after her, she thought, with a stab of guilt. *I can't blame it all on Granny.*

Pete sighed and shrugged her shoulders. "Have it your own way." She shut the flowered curtains around her bed. Her sulk hung over the cubicle like a black cloud.

Dulcie touched Flora's arm. "Give me your stocking and I'll darn it. Sewing's the only subject I'm good at."

"And we'll have another look at the spellbook." Pogo went to her secret hiding place, and used her ruler to lever up the loose floorboard. She took the book out of the hiding place and brought it over to Flora.

The book didn't feel magic. It felt dirty and a little damp, and when you turned the pages there was a faint whiff of old trainers. Flora looked through it with a sinking heart. What they needed was a list of spells, like recipes, and this was mostly – as far as Flora could make out from the strange print – stuff about ploughing and weather, and curing weird diseases in pigs. The famous chapter about "summonings" contained only the rhyme that had summoned Flora, and nothing at all about sending her home.

"Here." Pogo held out a crumpled paper bag. "Have a pear drop, and don't worry about Pete. She'll come round eventually."

The atmosphere in the bedroom was subdued this evening. Flora sucked a sweet that tasted of nail-polish remover, and tilted the old book towards the light from the lamp. On the first page, she could make

86

out the outline of a name, written very faintly in pencil – "W. Beak".

"Hey, look at this." She showed it to Pogo. "Does that have anything to do with Dame Mildred Beak, d'you think?"

Pogo and Dulcie were both fascinated. Pete stayed stubbornly quiet behind her cubicle curtains, but Flora somehow knew she was listening.

"This house was the home of the Beak family, before Dame Mildred turned it into a school," Pogo said. "W. Beak must be her father, Sir Wilberforce Beak – there's a portrait of the old chap above the library fireplace. I wonder if he was the person who collected all those books about magic?"

"Gosh," Dulcie said. "Do you think Dame Mildred knew?"

"I think she did – and it's rather obvious why she felt she had to hide them away when she opened a school," Pogo said ruefully. "She must've thought they'd be safe in the secret room. Oh, I wish she'd been right! Well, there's nothing else for it – we'll have to go back. It's all we can do. We're not going to find any magic anywhere else."

"Good," Flora said, "I'd like to take a look at that room. When shall we do it?"

"Well, next time there's a rainy half holiday—"

"But this is urgent! I can't wait till then!"

"Terribly sorry and all that, but it looks as if you'll have to. It doesn't help anyone if we get ourselves expelled, does it?"

This was perfectly reasonable, and there was no point in arguing. "OK."

"Look, shut up," a voice snapped behind the curtain. "Some people are trying to read!"

"I told you," Pogo said. "Ignore her."

Flora wished she could ignore Pete. After lights out, lying drowsily in her smooth, warm bed, she wondered what she had to do to make Pete accept her. The trouble was that Pete behaved like royalty. Dad would have called her "the Queen of Entitlement". She must be monumentally spoiled at home.

"Flora!" Dulcie whispered from the next bed. "Are you awake?"

"Yes," Flora whispered back.

"I forgot to ask — what's 'krupp'?"

"What? Oh, you mean cra— I'll tell you tomorrow."

"Is it — rude?"

"Yes."

Dulcie giggled softly. "Goodnight, then."

"Goodnight."

Dulcie said she was spoiled by her grandmother. But Dulcie was sweet and considerate, and did not behave like a spoiled person. Not like Pete, who always expected to get her own way.

And not like Flora.

On that terrible holiday in Italy, Flora had complained to Mum about the burden of looking after Ella.

"I thought it would be more fun if she was here too – and all she does is ask silly questions. And she's always reading!"

Mum had said, "It wouldn't do you any harm to read a book occasionally."

"Yes, but Ella reads when I want to talk to her!"

"She's your guest," Mum had said, "and it's not her job to amuse you."

Flora wished she had listened to this. It was too late to say sorry now, even if she did manage to get home.

8

Sink or Swim

Harbottle the Horrible began next morning's lesson with a massive attack on Pete. "Daphne Peterson, this is the absolute LAST STRAW! I ask for a simple exercise, and I get a tattered mess covered with blobs of ink!"

She was in a truly evil mood. Every girl in the class was shaking. Never had Flora missed APS so much. Modern teachers could be nasty, but not like this – Harbottle was going off like the villain in a James Bond film.

"For the whole of last term I endured work that looked like the trail of a DRUNKEN SLUG! This term I will make no more allowances!"

Flora stared down at her hands, clenched on top of her desk.

This is my fault, she thought uneasily. *Pete's homework wouldn't have been so bad if she hadn't had to do mine as well.*

"Careless! Slovenly!" Miss Harbottle chucked Pete's exercise book across the classroom like a Frisbee. "You will do it again – and if I don't see a mighty improvement, you will report to me for detention on Friday afternoon, directly after lunch. Consider yourself on probation."

"But—" Pete blurted out. She bit her lip and her face reddened.

"Oh, yes, Daphne, I am very well aware that the games captain is conducting trials for the hockey team on Friday. You'd better try not to miss it, hadn't you? Sit DOWN!"

Flora sneaked a glance at Pete. She was crazy about hockey, and already boasting that she would be chosen for the lower-school team. No wonder she looked gutted.

Books zoomed through the air as Miss Harbottle chucked them back at their owners. "Barbara Hardwick – ATROCIOUS! Cecilia Lawrence – not bad. Dorothy Sykes – not bad. Dulcie Latimer – dreadful as ever, but at least you TRIED!"

At last, only one book was left. "Flora Fox!" This time, she did not throw it. "Come here – right up to the front of the class!"

Flora hadn't expected this. She was a new girl, and teachers were supposed to make allowances if you were new. She stood up, on legs that were shaking, and went to the front of the class. Harbottle's wizened little face reminded her of a horrible shrunken head she had once seen in the British Museum.

"Flora Fox, if you were not a new gel, you would be most severely punished for this DISGRACEFUL piece of work!" She flipped open the exercise book, and showed the whole class the homework Pete was supposed to have done for her – half a page of pencilled scribbles.

Flora was furious. She glared at Pete, and the lazy cow didn't even look sorry.

"I shall be keeping my eye upon you, Flora Fox. It is my mission in life to root out insolent gels of your type. You will of course write out these verbs again. And then you will recite them to me from memory, tomorrow morning. Sit DOWN!"

Flora spent the rest of the lesson burning with embarrassment and anger. Thanks to Pete, the other girls in the class now thought she was completely stupid. She grabbed Pete at morning break, when they all surged into the lower-school common room for milk and biscuits.

"You messed up my homework! Now I've got to learn a load of Latin verbs!"

"Sorry, and all that," Pete said. "I clean forgot about

it until this morning, so I had to do it in the cloakroom."

"Thanks a lot! Try and put a bit more effort into it next time!"

"Next time? Do you think I'm doing any more of your prep for you? I've got enough of my own – I'll die if I miss the try-outs for the team!"

Flora was outraged. She had to keep her voice low, but it quivered with anger. "You promised to help me!"

"Nobody can learn things by heart for you," Pogo pointed out. "That's one thing you'll have to do for yourself."

"Yes, and that's going to take me the whole evening! Someone's just going to have to deal with the rest."

The other three looked at each other.

Pogo said, "The thing is, one of the teachers is bound to notice if we're doing your prep. They know our handwriting. It might be easier all round if you did your own. We'll help, of course."

"And I'll still do your darning," Dulcie added.

"But you have to deal with my work!" Flora hissed. "You promised!"

Pete groaned rudely. "I know – I know – because we brought you here. But even if we hadn't summoned you, you'd still have to go to school, wouldn't you? And even schools in the next century must make you do some sort of work."

"There isn't any homework at Penrice Hall."

"I'm sick of Penrice Hall. I don't believe it even exists! Pogo and Dulcie can do your prep if they want – but I simply don't have time."

This was awful. All Flora could say was, "But you promised!"

"That was before I knew how stupid and ignorant you future-girls are."

"Flora's not stupid!" Dulcie cried. "It's not her fault she doesn't know anything!"

She meant to be kind, but Flora was hurt. They all assumed that all "future-girls" were stupid, and all schools in the twenty-first century were rubbish.

And that's my fault, she thought, *because I've been so lazy and stroppy since I came here. I'm not exactly an advertisement for APS.*

"Even if we don't actually do your prep, we'll still help you as much as we can," Dulcie assured her.

"You only have to do the easiest parts," Pogo said. "And of course we'll keep telling you how to fit in, and so on."

She spoke politely, but Flora got the message loud and clear. They all thought she was a moron, and they were sick of looking after her. She drew herself up proudly. "Please don't bother. I'll manage perfectly well on my own."

"Steady on," Pogo said. "Is that wise? There seems to

be such a lot you don't know. And you have to pass as a schoolgirl from 1935."

"I can easily do that – what's so brilliant about you 1930s girls, anyway? You might laugh at me because I've never heard of the Battle of Blenheim, but at least I know about the war and the moon landings!"

"Moon landings?" Pete let out a bellow of laughter. "Now I KNOW you're making it all up!"

"Do people live on the moon in the future?" Pogo asked, interested. "Who colonized it? Us, I suppose."

"She made it up, you drip," Pete said, with withering scorn. "Nobody lives on the moon, and it's not made of green cheese, either. I vote we forget this whole future business, and leave Flora to sink or swim!"

"Fine – I don't need any of you!" Flora grabbed her satchel and stormed out of the common room. Her fury did not die down until she was out in the corridor, being swept along in a crowd of girls she didn't know. She realized what she had done. Without her three guards – the only people who knew about her coming from the future – she was officially the loneliest person in the universe.

The first lesson was English, and that wasn't too bad. The teacher, Miss Palmer, was quite young and wore a flowered dress under her gown, instead of the usual tweed suit and tie. She had written a poem on the blackboard. The girls all stood with their hands behind their backs, chanting it aloud in perfect unison:

"This is the weather the cuckoo likes,

And so do I;

When showers betumble the chestnut spikes,

And nestlings fly—"

Lunch, however, was an ordeal. Flora was in the middle of a chattering crowd, but nobody spoke to her. She might as well have been invisible. Dulcie gave her a pleading look and patted the chair beside her, and Flora nearly gave in – but Pete was pretending she didn't exist. She turned her face away angrily and dropped into the first spare seat she saw.

"Look who it is," said Consuela Carver. "Lo, the poor Indian!"

Flora frowned down at her plate of shepherd's pie and cabbage. It was just her luck to end up bang opposite the Carver. She'd have to try to ignore her.

"She's far too ashamed to open her mouth," the Carver told the table. "She doesn't want us to hear that frightful chichi accent – no wonder they had to send her to England!" She tittered nastily, and added, in what was meant to be cockney, "This is the weather wot the cuckoo likes!"

A few girls giggled.

"Lawks!" someone said.

"Cor blimey!" said someone else.

More giggling. Flora was surprised. Was this how she sounded – like someone in *EastEnders*? She'd always thought her speaking voice was rather posh. The other girls here all spoke with incredibly posh, old-fashioned voices – just like Granny, who said "thenk you" and "perheps" and "gorn".

"Do tell us, *Florrie*," the Carver said smoothly. "Is your mother a charwoman?"

Now she expects me to burst into tears, Flora thought. She knew that "charwoman" meant the same as "cleaning lady". "No," she said, looking the Carver straight in the eye, "but so what if she was? I wouldn't care. Only snobs care about things like that."

The Carver's face reddened with annoyance. "If my parents wanted me educated with the daughters of charwomen, they'd have sent me to a council school!"

Flora held up one hand, and said in her best imitation of Granny, "Talk to the HEND – the face jolly well doesn't care!"

Consuela was flabbergasted. There was a long moment of silence. Someone giggled – but not at Flora.

A voice down the table muttered, "Good for the maggot – how priceless!"

Consuela's eyes narrowed, and she stared at Flora with real dislike. This piece of twenty-first-century rudeness had made Flora a serious enemy. At this moment, she didn't care. Pete couldn't help looking impressed, and that was what counted.

Going solo wasn't easy. On that lonely first evening, Flora found a spare place at one of the tables in the lower-school common room and sat down to tackle her 1930s homework.

At APS she usually got a printed worksheet. At St Winifred's there was more learning by heart. She had the Latin verbs to write out and learn (present indicative: *sum*, *es*, *est*, *sumus*, *estis*, *sunt*; imperfect indicative: *eram*, *eras*, *erat*, *eramus*, *eratis*, *erant*), and also the first two verses of the cuckoo poem. Flora rather enjoyed writing with the other Flora's fountain pen, though you had to be careful not to get covered with ink.

When the prep was done, the other two girls at the table struck up a friendly conversation. It was nice, though pretending she was a 1930s girl was hard work. Flora did her best to concentrate on the memories of the other Flora (she was getting quite a knack for this), and managed to answer questions without looking too thick.

Their names were Jill Scott and Bunty (short for Barbara) Hardwick. Jill was short, with thick brown hair and millions of freckles. Bunty was tall and thin, with goofy teeth (at home in the future, she would've had elaborate braces on her teeth, like Ella's).

"We ought to be chums," Jill said. "I'm from India too. Are your people army or civil service?"

"Army."

"We're civil service. Where are you stationed?"

"Poona."

"We're in Bombay. Have a toffee."

By the time the bell rang for lower-school bedtime, Flora had been the other Flora for so long that she had almost forgotten the future. The twenty-first century came rushing back to her in the cloakroom. It was the Bluebells' night for baths, and she would have given half her tuck box for a hot shower at home – with shampoo and shower gel and conditioner.

If you could believe it, the baths here had lines drawn round the insides, to show the amount of water you were allowed. Flora washed herself and her hair in a few lukewarm inches. It was extremely difficult to rinse the shampoo out of her hair without a shower attachment. She came out of the cubicle shivering like a dog in the rain.

Needless to say, there was no such thing as a hairdryer, and the soap smelled of public toilets. But she was not going to complain. Pete had left her to sink or swim, and Flora was determined to swim. She would show them all what future-girls were made of, starting with that witch Harbottle.

On her last night at home in Wimbledon, she had

fallen asleep with her iPod stuck in her ears. On her fourth night at St Winifred's, she fell asleep muttering Latin verbs.

Amare – to love. *Amo*, *amas*, *amat*, *amamus*, *amatis* . . .

9

Portia

"By the end of this lesson," Pete said, in a tragic voice, "my life may be in ruins. If Harbottle doesn't like my prep, I'll miss the trials – and I know I'm good enough for the lower-school team!"

"Do stop worrying," Dulcie said soothingly. "Of course you'll be in the team."

"I sort of HAVE to be – I've already told my people."

"Hmm," Pogo said, with a wry glance at Flora. "That was counting your chickens a bit, wasn't it?"

Pete snorted crossly. "How did I know Harbottle would try to ruin everything?"

They were back in the classroom after morning break. Pete was at her desk, with the redone homework in front of her, anxiously checking it one more time.

Despite being so cross with Pete, Flora couldn't help sympathizing. Pete had totally slaved over that homework. Being tidy was harder for her than it was for everyone else, and a teacher from the future would never have picked on her.

"Oh, what a pity you won't make the hockey trials!" sighed Consuela Carver, strolling past Pete's desk.

"Who says I won't?" growled Pete.

"Well, if Harbottle doesn't like your prep – oh – WHOOPS!"

Pete let out a howl of anguish.

The Carver had been fiddling with her fountain pen, and she suddenly sprayed a shower of blue ink across Pete's homework. "SO sorry!"

"You minger!" Flora gasped. "You did that on purpose!"

"I'm afraid I don't speak Indian," the Carver said. "No understandee!"

Every girl in the class was watching now.

Pogo said, "Of course you'll own up to Miss Harbottle."

"Own up?" snapped the Carver. "Whatever for? Her work's awful anyway – a few blots won't make much difference."

There were a few sharp breaths at this, and someone whistled.

Consuela looked defiantly at the whistler. "You can

102

tell her if you like, Bunty Hardwick – if you're a beastly SNEAK! You know how the Harbottle despises a sneak."

Everyone went quiet and still. Pete's head was hanging, and her ears were scarlet. She was trying very hard not to cry. Dulcie was mopping up the worst of the ink with a piece of blotting paper, but the homework was still a mess.

Flora couldn't believe this was happening. "You're just going to let her get away with it?"

Pogo muttered, "Shh! You don't understand—"

"Well, I don't see what's so bad about being a sneak – I'll tell her!"

This time, there was a universal gasp and (from the Carver and her friends) hisses of "Sneak! You wouldn't dare!"

The door banged open, and all the girls turned to statues as Miss Harbottle stalked into the classroom.

"*Salvete!*"

The class chorused "*Salve!*" (Pogo had explained to Flora that this meant "hello".)

"Sit DOWN."

They all sat down. Harbottle swept her glinty little eyes across the class. "Daphne Peterson!"

Pete stood up. Her lips formed the words, "Yes, Miss Harbottle."

"Bring me your book."

Pete picked up her exercise book and slowly took it to the front of the class. Harbottle snatched it with her small, wrinkled claw, and stared at Pete's spoiled work for what seemed like ages.

"This is worse than carelessness," she said eventually. "This is out-and-out INSOLENCE! I will not have my patience tried by insolent, LAZY little gels! You will report to my study, directly after lunch."

The blow had fallen. Pete bowed her head. She wasn't even trying to look brave.

It was so incredibly unfair that Flora couldn't bear it. She jumped to her feet. "Excuse me, Miss Harbottle, but it wasn't her fault!"

"I BEG your pardon?" Harbottle was outraged.

"It's not fair, that's all. Pete – Daphne – shouldn't have detention, because it wasn't her fault that her homework got covered with ink."

"Really? Whose fault was it?"

Flora looked round. Everyone was staring at her. Dulcie looked appalled, and the Carver was trying not to smirk. The fact was that even in the twenty-first century, you still didn't grass up your classmates, no matter how nasty they were. There was only one thing she could say.

"It was my fault – I did it."

This caused a sensation. Nobody made a sound, but the atmosphere was electric.

Harbottle stared at her coldly, for what seemed like ages. "You?"

"Yes."

A flurry of underground whispers ran through the class. "Own up!"

Consuela folded her arms and tried to look as if she didn't care – though her cheeks were redder than usual.

"Why couldn't Daphne have told me this herself?"

"Because you despise sneaks."

"I do," said Harbottle. "And I suppose I should commend you for owning up. But I can't help knowing that you are a crony of Miss Peterson's, and I wouldn't be at all surprised if you had arranged this whole charade between you, to disguise her atrocious handiwork. Sit DOWN!"

Flora was dismayed – this was totally backfiring. Suddenly, she didn't care what trouble she got into. She had to put it right. "Look, Miss Harbottle, I swear I didn't do it on purpose – everyone here knows I'm telling the truth. If you want to give me another punishment, that's fine. This isn't about me. The point is that Pete – Daphne, I mean – shouldn't have detention. She worked very hard at that homework. If you look underneath the blots, the actual work is fine."

Miss Harbottle's astonished outrage had changed to ordinary nastiness. "Good gracious, child, why should

105

I trouble to look under the blots? Daphne's work is ALWAYS atrocious!"

"Not this time – as you'd see if you looked properly."

The rest of the class were gawping at Flora as if she had put her head between the jaws of a dragon, but Flora suddenly felt braver. Miss Harbottle was not shouting out insults, but looking at her very thoughtfully.

"Interesting," she said. "And what do you think I should do about this situation?"

Feeling she had nothing left to lose, Flora said, "I don't know. I just know it's not fair on Pe – Daphne."

"Hmmmm. You are very sure of yourself, Miss Fox." Harbottle came over to Flora, and stood devouring her with those sharp, black eyes. "Why, I wonder, do I feel I'm not hearing the whole story?"

"I don't know."

"Are you covering up for someone?"

"I'm trying to make sure Pete – Daphne – doesn't get in trouble because someone else is a bully." It was very uncomfortable, being so close to the watchful, wrinkled face. "At my other school – I mean, the one I used to go to – we all had to sign an anti-bullying charter, and if someone's a bully, you're actually supposed to tell on them."

"Your other school?"

"Y-yes." Flora had forgotten about the other Flora's

106

governess, but there was no going back now. She remembered something Mr Burton, the headmaster of APS, had said in one of his assemblies last term. "If you give in to bullies, you just perpetuate the culture of bullying."

"Fascinating," said Miss Harbottle. "You're quite the barrack-room lawyer, Flora Fox." To Flora's surprise, there was a gleam in the little black eyes that might have been amusement. She seemed not to hear the whispers of "Own up, you beast!" that were hissing round Consuela. "You have put your case eloquently, if not elegantly. Daphne, you will NOT have detention. As the poem says, *Curfew shall not ring tonight*."

Pete's tearful face lit up all over with joy, and she gave Flora a radiant smile.

"As for you, Flora, since you are fond of making courtroom speeches, you will spend your free time this Saturday and Sunday learning one by Shakespeare – Portia's famous speech from *The Merchant of Venice*, beginning 'The quality of mercy is not strained'. You will recite it to me on Monday morning, instead of the Latin verbs. Sit DOWN."

"Yes, Miss Harbottle." The Shakespeare sounded tough, but Flora was too happy to care. Pete was her friend again, and it felt lovely.

"I know I've been a beast to you," Pete said. "You were

a brick to stand up for me, and I'm sorry I was so – so—"

"Selfish," suggested Pogo.

"Shut up! I'm trying to apologize, and you know how I hate it! Look here, Flora, shall we call it pax?"

"That means 'peace'," Dulcie said helpfully. "It's Latin."

"I'd love to call it pax," Flora said. They shook hands (1930s girls did not hug), and Dulcie gave them all a piece of fudge to celebrate.

It made a great end to this stormy day. The four of them had managed to bag the two big armchairs beside the common-room gas fire. Flora and Pogo sat together in one chair, Pete lounged in the other, and Dulcie sat on the rug at their feet. They had spent the grey, drizzly afternoon shivering on the hockey field, and Pete – to her joy – had been chosen for the lower-school team. Rhoda Pugh, the games captain, had even called her a "promising youngster". She had added, "But don't forget your team spirit, will you? A good team player never plays just for herself."

Which is exactly what Pete does, Flora thought. *It's a pity she didn't listen to that bit.*

But she was friends with Pete again, and nothing else mattered. It felt almost as good as if she had made up with Ella. The hot fire and the cosy shabbiness of the room made Flora feel warm and safe. A lot of the girls had gone to choir practice (the choir could be heard across the hall, singing a song called "The Wild Brown Bee is My Lover") and the Common Room was half empty.

"You're quite a heroine, Flora," Dulcie said. "Everyone's talking about it. And they're all disgusted with the Carver. She's a bully, just like Flashman in *Tom Brown's Schooldays*."

"Steady on," Pogo said. "She hasn't roasted anyone over an open fire yet."

"She would if she could," Pete said darkly.

"Pete," Dulcie said, "have you gone back to believing Flora's from the future?"

"Oh, crikey." Pete had the good grace to look ashamed. "I didn't really stop believing it. I was just so boiling mad about the extra prep. Sorry, Flora. I swear I'll atone for it now. I'll let you go on about computators and portable telephones as much as you like."

"Thanks," said Flora.

Dulcie said, "We promised we'd help her to get home."

Flora was touched – it was like Dulcie to remember a promise. She was also a little guilty that she had almost forgotten about wanting to go home. Of course she did. She had to get home.

"I don't want to send you away," Pete said, giving Flora one of her brilliant smiles. "Why don't you stay for a bit?"

"Pete, you really are the pink limit," Pogo said, chuckling. "She isn't here to amuse you. Perhaps we should have yet another look at the spellbook – though I wish I knew why Flora's spell worked and none of the others did."

"I vote we have another go at making the Carver bald," Pete said. "We left out the cobweb last time."

"That's because it's impossible to carry a cobweb in your pocket," Dulcie said. "It just sort of disappears."

"Watch out," Pogo said suddenly.

Consuela Carver had come into the room. She was scowling. She walked stiffly up to the four girls. "I've come to apologize," she said furiously. "I inked your work on purpose, and – and – I'm sorry."

Pete said, "You don't look particularly sorry."

"That's because I'm not," the Carver said sulkily. "I'm only doing it because Harbottle told me to."

"Harbottle?" Pogo was surprised.

"Yes. Thanks to Pete and that vulgar little beast from India, I had to spend the whole afternoon with her, being lectured about ladylike behaviour. Please don't imagine you've heard the last of this." She whisked round and stomped out of the room.

"Well I never," Pogo said thoughtfully. "It's not like Harbottle to get involved in something like this."

"Huh," sniffed Pete. "The Carver's not very good at apologizing!"

"Crikey, look who's talking," Pogo said. "Do try not to put her back up, Pete. It'll only make more trouble for Flora."

"I can handle her," Flora said. Standing up to Harbottle had given her confidence. She didn't care if Carver thought she was a vulgar little beast. "I've decided to carry on managing on my own. It's not that I don't want to be friends with you lot," she added hastily. "But we don't know how long I'll have to stay here, do we? And this school isn't as horrible as I thought. I've decided to try to get used to it."

"I call that jolly brave," Dulcie said warmly. "Have another piece of fudge."

"I call it sensible," Pogo said. "Of course we'll help you whenever you need it — but I have a feeling you won't be needing us much. I'd say you future-girls are made of pretty good stuff."

10

A Discovery

Flora worked hard at settling in. Over the next couple of weeks, thanks to the memories of the other Flora, the lessons began to seem less puzzling, and her own knowledge from the twenty-first century turned out to be surprisingly useful. She astonished Miss Fosdyke, who taught botany and science, with the amount she knew about the solar system.

"I'm most impressed, Flora. You have evidently made a serious study of astronomy."

If only she knew, Flora thought, that at home I can summon up the entire galaxy on my computer screen.

It was good to know that she wasn't stupid. The other girls were better at things like verbs and times tables and historical dates. But Flora, who watched the

Discovery Channel and Animal Planet at home, and often browsed through Wikipedia on her computer, was able to reel off facts about all sorts of interesting things – earthquakes, volcanoes, the life cycle of the penguin and the dinosaurs of the Jurassic age. The magic might have blocked off certain things, but she had no trouble remembering all this, and she began to get good marks in geography and science.

In private, Pogo was wild with envy. "I'd give my eye teeth to see that film about earthquakes – and the one about the inside of a meerkat's house – and the close-up pictures of the moons of Jupiter. You future-girls are so lucky!"

Yes, they were rather lucky. The more Flora got used to the past, the more she appreciated all the things in the future that she had always taken for granted – things like hot showers, television, computers, microwaves, iPods and decent hair products. Everyone in the 1930s had appalling hair. Because they hardly ever washed it, it was either lank and stringy, or frizzy.

Even without products, something had to be done. One evening, armed with nothing but sharp scissors, a comb and a bowl of water, Flora gave her three friends a makeover.

"I wish you lot could see my proper hair – at home in the future, I have a kind of spiky, layered cut, and blonde streaks."

"Gosh, you dyed your hair!" gasped Dulcie. "Weren't your people furious?"

"Course not – it was one of my birthday presents. Everyone has dyed hair in the future. If Old Peepy lived in the future, she'd dye her hair to cover up all that grey. And she'd do something about her eyebrows."

Flora was working on an unwilling Pogo. She undid her two short, thin pigtails, and carefully snipped her hair into a shoulder-length bob with a fringe.

When she had finished, Pogo stared at herself in the mirror for ages, without saying a word.

"You look – different," Dulcie said. "Actually, you look awfully nice."

"It doesn't feel quite right, that's all," Pogo said doubtfully. "My mother and father would say I was being vain. My father's a bishop, don't forget. He doesn't approve of vanity."

"What about me?" Pete demanded. "How would my hair look in the future?"

Pete's shambolic dark hair was more of a challenge. Flora flattened it with a wet comb, and did her best to trim the edges so that it looked a little neater. If only she'd had her hair straighteners – but Pete was delighted, and even Pogo relaxed her disapproval. "I say, Pete, you look almost human!"

Dulcie picked up one of her own blonde plaits. "Do

all future-people have short hair? Should I cut off my plaits?"

"No way!" Flora said firmly. "Your hair's gorgeous – you don't do enough with it. Why not wear it loose?"

"It's against the rules."

"Long hair must be neatly tied back," Pogo said, grinning, "in case it escapes and gets into the custard!"

Flora was a little annoyed that she couldn't send Dulcie down to breakfast in the morning with a glorious blonde mane. Pete and Pogo, however, created a sensation – especially Pogo, whose peaky little face was transformed by the flattering fringe. Mademoiselle Dornay, the French teacher, grabbed her chin and said, "*Tiens, c'est jolie!*" And several girls asked Flora if they could have makeovers too.

Suddenly, Flora was a success. People stopped treating her like the village idiot. She wrote an essay about life in the twenty-first century, in which she tried to explain modern things in a way that people in the 1930s would understand. She worked extremely hard at it, even in her free time when she could have been finishing *The Secret Garden* (which turned out to be the best book of all time – what a shame she couldn't discuss it with Ella – Mary was SO going to marry Dickon when she grew up) and Miss Bradley said she would publish it in the school magazine.

"Most imaginative, Flora – I especially liked the

super-oven that splits atoms and heats food in a few seconds. Between ourselves, I could do with one in my study!"

The only teacher who didn't like the essay was Miss Harbottle. "All very well," she croaked, "but I don't trust a gel with too much imagination. Imagination is very bad for gels."

Flora wished Harbottle would get off her back – the old witch always seemed to be watching her suspiciously. As far as everyone else was concerned, however, Flora was doing very well. She spoke French at breakfast. She sang the hymns in assembly. She wrote polite letters to the other Flora's parents. She played hockey. She learned to darn, hemstitch and make buttonholes. To the naked eye, she was a normal schoolgirl of the 1930s.

But of course, she wasn't. The 1930s schoolgirl was a shell, with a twenty-first century girl hiding inside her, and her friends had not forgotten their promise to find a way of sending her home. When the term was a few weeks old there was a half holiday in honour of Dame Mildred Beak's birthday, and – even better – it was pouring with rain.

"We're allowed to wander round the house when it rains," Pogo explained. "The attics are still out of bounds, but nobody will notice if we sneak upstairs. We couldn't have better conditions for another raid on the secret room."

Flora's heart gave a leap of hope. She was getting used to the past, and even liking some bits of it, but the longing to go home nagged at her like a toothache. She couldn't wait to search the secret room.

In the morning they had a special assembly, with a prayer of thanksgiving for the life of Dame Mildred, and a girl from the lower sixth played the violin. The head girl, Audrey Biggins, solemnly placed a big vase of spring flowers on the mantelpiece under Dame Mildred's stern portrait in the hall. This was followed by the usual morning school, then lunch.

In the afternoon the rain still poured. The girls had to amuse themselves indoors, and the old house resounded with shrieks of laughter and the sound of pounding feet and slamming doors. Old Peepy believed it was sometimes necessary for girls to let off a little steam, and the teachers kindly kept their distance.

The four girls found Ethel, and asked if they could use her bedroom window.

"Go on, then," Ethel said. "Just don't go killing yourselves. Are you looking for magic again?" She was laughing at them. "Bring back a nice spell for me."

"What kind of spell would you like?" Dulcie asked seriously.

"A rich husband, please."

"We'll do our best."

"She doesn't believe us," Flora said, when they were

hurrying upstairs. "Wouldn't it be great if we really found her a rich husband?"

Dulcie sighed romantically. "It'd be just like *King Cophetua and the Beggar-maid!* That's a picture I have in my bedroom at home."

"I'd rather have a handsome husband," Pete said.

The stairs and corridors swarmed with girls. In their bedroom corridor, some second-formers were having a lively game of cricket, using rolled-up stockings as a ball. Nobody noticed the four girls darting up to the attic floor, where the servants slept under the eaves.

Ethel's door was at the end of a narrow passage, and beside it was the flat piece of wall where the door to the hidden room had been bricked up. Flora touched it curiously.

Pogo had brought her shoe bag, to carry any promising books or papers. She slung this over her shoulder. "Dulcie, you don't like crawling along gutters – you stay here and keep cave."

"Righto."

"If you hear anyone coming, thump on the wall."

"Righto – then what?"

"Use your initiative," Pogo said.

"My – what?"

"Never mind, there isn't time. Come on, you two – we should aim to be out before the bell for tea."

Flora followed Pogo and Pete into Ethel's tiny

bedroom. Pete wriggled out through the small dormer window and Pogo nimbly crawled after her. From where Flora stood, it looked as if they were about to fall over the stone rail outside and plunge to the ground. When it was her turn, however, she saw that it wasn't as dangerous as it appeared. The gutter was very broad, and though the stone rail was low, it would be hard to fall unless you were standing up. All the same, she didn't dare to look down.

It was raining hard. Flora spent an unpleasant couple of minutes on her hands and knees in the gutter, with the rain drumming down on her back. By the time she crawled into the secret room, she was wet and shivering.

The secret room was a bit of a disappointment. Flora had pictured something dark and cluttered and full of mystery, but this was simply a small, bare room with a sloping ceiling, furnished with three plain wooden boxes. Dust lay everywhere, in drifts and puffs and swirls. And there was an odd atmosphere – not exactly creepy, but Flora had a sense of a personality, or the memory of one, and she couldn't decide if it was good or bad.

They took a box each. Pogo doggedly sifted through every single paper in the third box, putting the few papers that were in English into her shoe bag. Flora went through the old books. These were very old and heavy, and – as they had told her – mostly in Latin and various unknown scripts. Pete poked about in the box that was full of glass bottles and tubes. She soon got bored, and started making patterns in the dust with her feet.

"This looks promising." Pogo held up a small, shabby school notebook.

"Huh," said Pete. "Someone's old homework."

"Golly – it's a lot better than that!" Pogo was excited. "Look!" She showed them the faded, looped writing on the cover: "Private Experiments". She opened the notebook, and slowly read the small, neat handwriting. "1st November 1875. Today I commence my private record of certain experiments in Alchemy, Sorcery and Witchcraft, using books from the secret library amassed by my late father, Sir Wilberforce Beak."

She stopped. The three girls stared at each other. Flora started shivering again.

"Dame Mildred's diary!" Pete said slowly. "How funny that we found it on her birthday."

"We can't read it now, the light's going," Pogo said. "And – I don't quite know why – but I'd rather like to get out of here."

Flora knew what she meant. You couldn't put your finger on it, but something in the atmosphere made her very uneasy. She was glad to leave this strange, uncanny room and crawl back along the gutter. A few minutes later, they burst out of Ethel's bedroom to show the diary to Dulcie.

"I vote we go up to the bedroom directly after tea," Pogo said, her eyes shining through a mask of dust. "Thank goodness it's a half holiday and there's no prep."

Dulcie giggled. "You'd better clean off some of that dirt – you look as if you've been up the chimney!"

Flora, Pogo and Pete suddenly noticed the state they were all in and burst out laughing. They were covered with dust that the rain had turned to mud. Pete had a beard of dirt, and one of Flora's stockings had fallen down. Far below them the bell rang for tea, and they all pelted down to the cloakroom to scrub off the worst of it – Dulcie kindly came with them to help.

They were late for tea, and Pete had the misfortune to run smack into Mademoiselle Dornay, who crossly gave her "*un pony*".

"Krupp!" Pete swore. "I do have the most awful rotten luck!"

The "krupp" nearly made Flora choke on her tea – Pete certainly loved rude words, and she decided she'd try not to let out any more, or where would it end?

"Do hurry up, Dulcie!" hissed Pogo. "That's your third piece of cake."

"I can't help it if I'm hungry. If I eat any faster I'll choke."

The four girls were free to run up to their bedroom as soon as Dulcie had stopped eating. Though Flora was eager to discover the secrets of Dame Mildred's private diary, she was enjoying herself today. It was fun to run around and talk in a loud, unladylike voice, and generally behave more like a girl from the twenty-first century.

Just as they were going into Bluebell, Jill Scott leapt out of Eglantine and smacked Pete in the face with a pillow.

"OW! Bedroom battle!" roared Pete.

As Dulcie hurriedly explained, this meant they had been challenged to a pillow fight. Flora rushed into the bedroom with the others, to grab her pillow. There were no rules to the pillow fight, but it was hilarious – Flora managed to give Bunty Hardwick a tremendous whack on the bottom, and Pete laughed so much, she had to lie down on the floor. Two other bedrooms joined the fray, and the corridor was a riot of girls and white pillows, all shrieking blue murder. Pete and Flora barricaded three girls inside Japonica, and Pogo saved Dulcie from being taken hostage in Lily.

It only stopped when Miss Bradley waded in. "All right, you hooligans – that was the bell, so kindly put up your pillows and sign a peace treaty!"

At last, the four girls were settled in a solemn circle on the bedroom floor. Pogo, who was best at making out Dame Mildred's faint writing, held the diary under the light of the lamp and began to read.

Diary of an Amateur Sorceress

1st November 1875

*Today I commence my private record of certain
experiments in Alchemy, Sorcery and Witchcraft, using
books from the secret library amassed by my late father,
Sir Wilberforce Beak. I did not know about the books
until I found them after his death. He left instructions
to burn them, but I have decided to ignore him, in the
interests of Science. The time is right for a serious study
of the crafts too often left in the hands of cranks and
fools.*

*The most practical volume is unquestionably the
small, crude book of traditional country spells.
(Father's notes: published 1638 — he bought it for
sixpence off an old dame in the village.) This is the only
evidence I have seen of the lost knowledge of the
peasantry.*

This evening, I locked myself in my study and tried a simple spell for making water boil without a fire. Following instructions, I placed a quart of cold water in an earthenware bowl on the floor. Using a compass, I positioned myself facing exactly eastwards, took a sprig of lavender in either hand, and recited the incantation.

> "Blister and boil
> Till steam doth coil,
> Till air is mist,
> By sweet herbs kist – et cetera

RESULT: Nothing. Temperature of water remained constant throughout.

OBSERVATIONS: It is possible that my feeling very foolish when doing the above spoiled the effect of the magic.

2nd ATTEMPT: Tried again, lowering voice to dramatic stage whisper.

RESULT: Again, nothing.

OBSERVATIONS: Either this is all so much moonshine, or I am doing something wrong.

3rd ATTEMPT: This time, no play-acting. I said the spell as if giving an order to a member of staff. A person of my distinction cannot be at the mercy of any force, real or imaginary. The moment I took command, a kind

*of strength entered me like an arrow, shot through me
and poured from the ends of my fingers.*

*RESULT: Water boiled merrily. Made a pot of excellent
tea.*

*OBSERVATIONS: This appears to be a crude method of
harnessing an unknown power by force of personality.*

23rd November 1875
*Further experiments delayed by the distractions of
overseeing a school. Poor Celeste H. ran away again,
and many anxious hours passed before she was
returned to us by a policeman. Her mother died last
year and she does not want to live with her father's
new wife. She ran away when she heard she was to
be sent home. Her dearest wish is to stay at school,
but Mr H. will not hear of it. He does not see the
point of educating a girl, even when she is as promising
as Celeste. He says she will leave us at Easter, as
soon as he and his wife are returned from their
wedding journey. Celeste is resigned to doing her
duty as a daughter, but very downcast.*

*Another successful experiment – made a jug of fresh
milk turn sour and (much harder, needing greater
strength of will) I then made it turn fresh again.*

*A very practical and handy spell, particularly in
warm weather. And the spell for making water boil*

*would be most welcome at a picnic. I am hoping,
however, to benefit humanity – to cast spells that will
heal and help. Can I find a spell to help Celeste?*

5th January 1876
*Girls return on the 10th. At last, a chance to prepare for
an important experiment. The idea of a "summoning"
fascinates me. Dare I attempt to summon a "demon"
from the future? Even supposing such a thing possible,
what form might the demon take? I remember some
highly questionable "occult" pictures left by Father,
which I burned at the first opportunity. I cannot
summon anything that might not be suitable for a girls'
school.*

6th January
Feast of the Epiphany – not a day for sorcery.

10th January
*First day of term. The usual chaos of half the girls
weeping and the other half behaving as if still at home.
And the noise! Too vexed to know whether I am running
a school or a zoo.*

11th January
*A very strange thing happened this afternoon. I tried a
spell to increase the amount of milk produced by cows on*

the estate farm. In the middle, realized I was being watched, and discovered Celeste H. peeping at me through the keyhole. I was very angry, and the poor child was terrified. Despite her terror, however, she could not help asking questions, and those questions were so intelligent that I thought of a perfect way to guarantee her silence. Celeste is now my assistant. Under my direction, she measured the herbs and read the incantation for the milk spell.

What a peculiar little thing she is, with those eyes like round black buttons, and a perfect haystack of fuzzy black hair!

12th January

I was right to enlist Celeste. Perhaps because she is young, she appears to have a natural gift for magic. Early this morning I walked to the dairy, and the dairyman told me the cows had yielded a great deal more milk than usual (exact words: "They're spurting out this morning fit to drown you").

In the evening, when Celeste came to my study for her Greek lesson, I told her about the "summoning" spell. She seized the idea eagerly, begging me to try the spell on her. I began to tell her of my doubts, but she would not hear them. Till the day I die, I shall recall her exact words: "If we summon a future demon to help me, I know it'll find a way to let me stay at school!" I warned *her that it would be difficult, perhaps dangerous, but there is a stubborn spirit inside that puny frame, and she kept on at me until I relented.*

We are to carry out the summoning during Celeste's next Greek lesson, the day after tomorrow. I am curious, and a little nervous.

14th January
This was an experience to chill the blood. I have barely recovered, and will have to drink some brandy before I can face any of my teaching staff or servants.

Celeste came to my study at five. I sat her down in a chair that faced due east and locked the door. The child was very still and very pale, but bravely determined to go through with it. I threw the hog's bristle, milk thistle, et cetera into the bowl. I could sense Celeste's longing, and it made me call up my utmost strength and authority as I chanted the spell.

A great wind rushed through the room, stirring heaps of papers on my desk and blowing Celeste's hair across her frightened face.

And then it appeared.

I nearly screamed aloud.

It was a dreadful figure, ghostly and transparent — a young woman in a man's costume, who seemed to be shouting something and looking very surprised. She was in the room for perhaps three minutes (frankly I was too terrified to take note of the time), and then she melted away.

Celeste fell off her chair in a dead faint. I saw then how selfish I had been, to use her in this way. How could I have done it, when I might have killed her? I revived her with smelling salts and water, assuring her that the demon had gone – but my nerves are at breaking point.

15th January

A queer development. The new teacher arrived today, a young woman named Elizabeth Mosse. The first sign that all was not well came after luncheon. Miss Craig told me Miss Mosse was causing an "uproar" in the Staff Common Room. She wants to cut her hair and to wear trousers like a man. She claims to be something called a "Veegan" and annoyed Cook very much by throwing a good pork chop into the bin.

How my heart sank when I heard all this. I asked Miss Craig to send the young woman to me. Miss Mosse barged in a few minutes later, without knocking. As I feared, she insists that she comes from the future. She is muddled about the details, but I am sure she is telling the truth. She kept using words like "Patriarchy" and "Oppression", and says she teaches something called Women's Studies at a University of which I have never heard. She was impertinent enough to suggest that I

129

needed to "raise my consciousness". I was firm, and told her that any more talk of this kind would force me to dismiss her.

Truth to tell, I am afraid of her. Is she mentally unbalanced – or is she the "demon" I summoned for Celeste? Should I have told her why she is here? It is the Governors' meeting tomorrow, and I must see that Miss Mosse is firmly kept out of the way.

16th January

Very nearly a disaster. Miss Mosse somehow managed to insinuate herself into my upstairs drawing room while the Governors were having tea. Hardly any of them noticed, thank goodness – too busy "scoffing" cakes, as the girls would say. To my horror, I found the woman deep in conversation with – of all people – my newest and most important School Governor, the young Countess of Matlock. Her Ladyship was gracious, and promised to pay a call on someone or other, but I was so annoyed, I nearly dragged Miss Mosse out of the room by her hair.

I fail to see how this sort of thing can help Celeste.

23rd January

A most astonishing letter this morning, from Mr H. He has changed his mind about education for girls, and now wishes Celeste to continue at St Winifred's. This was *such joyful news that it took me a minute or two to notice the oddness of the rest of the letter. Mr H. says the "scales fell from his eyes" when he and his wife were visited by the Countess of Matlock. This brilliant young noblewoman spoke with great eloquence about Celeste's excellent abilities, and he saw that it would be a sin to waste them. He is now such a keen supporter of female education that he has donated two hundred pounds to Lady Matlock's Evening School for Labouring Girls. I must admit that I absolutely fell back in my chair when I read this. Two hundred pounds! Has this spell of mine made everyone mad? I was longing to talk to Miss Mosse, to whom I owe an apology. First, however, I had to give Celeste the good news. I sent for her after breakfast and it was wonderful to behold the happiness dawning in that pinched, miserable face.*

She admitted that she had poured out her heart to Miss Mosse, and it had been Miss Mosse's idea to talk to Lady Matlock. Miss Mosse said that she had read about Lady Matlock in a book about women's history – apparently, in the future, Her Ladyship is revered as a great pioneer.

Naturally, this made me all the more eager to talk to Miss Mosse. But it was too late. Miss Craig came in, to say Miss Mosse was behaving "oddly". When Miss Mosse herself was brought to my study, I saw at once that a profound change had come over her.

She was no longer brazen and rude, but timid and dazed. She told me she thought she had been ill with a fever, during which she had experienced a terrible kind of "living nightmare".

In this nightmare she had been living one hundred years in the future, with a group of women who called themselves a "feminist collective". Miss Mosse said she was most distressed to find herself with her hair cut short, wearing trousers and some kind of long vest with the words "Women's Liberation" printed upon it. She also claims to have a met a lady who was a Member of Parliament.

I made the poor creature a herbal draught, to persuade her that this had been nothing more than a bad dream. I told her never to speak about it again, but after she had gone I was in a great state of excitement.

I have never seen why women should not have the same education as men, the same rights as men. I would like to be a Member of Parliament – but I do not even have a vote. These revelations from the future fill me with hope. Will I live to vote? Will my dear girls?

It is clear that the Miss Mosse from the future has returned to her own enlightened time, having set Celeste on course for a happier life. The Miss Mosse from the present now thinks she dreamed her stay in the 1970s, and everyone is in her right place. An entirely successful experiment — but an alarming one. It must be wrong to interfere with the workings of Providence in this way. I shall make no more experiments in this field.

"And that's all," Pogo said, into the breathless silence. "There isn't any more."

"Poor Celeste!" Dulcie whispered. "Imagine hating your home so much that you'd rather be at school!"

"Maybe her home life was happier, after her dad turned into a feminist," Flora suggested.

"Well, I think it's a bit of a swizz," Pete said crossly. "There isn't anything about how to get rid of a demon — the one Dame Mildred summoned vanished all by itself."

"Only when her task was completed," Pogo said. "Don't you see? That's the whole point. Celeste's demon helped her to stay at St Win's — and once she'd done that, she went back to her own time."

"Why haven't I gone back to mine?" Flora asked wistfully.

"Because you haven't done your task yet!"

"What task?"

Pogo shrugged. "I don't know. Let's assume you were sent to help Pete, since she was the one who chanted the spell. I suppose you'll know what it is when you see it. And when you've done it — saved Pete from a runaway train or something — you'll simply go home."

133

Flora thought about this. Deep down, she had dreamed that they would find a spell to send her home to the future that very night. It was disappointing that this was not going to happen. On the other hand, she now knew she would be going home eventually, and that was a great weight off her mind. She could concentrate on school without constantly worrying that she would never see her parents again. The other Elizabeth Mosse had gone home to her 1970s feminist collective, and she would go home to twenty-first century Wimbledon. How clever the summoning spell had been, to know that the best demon for Celeste would be a feminist historian, who knew about Lady Matlock being a brilliant pioneer, or whatever.

Why had the magic chosen Flora for Pete? And when would they know what Flora had come to do?

12

Half-term

n the meantime, the evenings were getting lighter, and it was coming up to half-term. At home in the future, half-term lasted for one week. Here it was just one day. Parents and friends were allowed to take the girls out. Pete's parents were driving all the way from London. Pogo's brother Neville was coming from Cambridge, and Dulcie's granny was coming from south Devon with Dorsey, who had once been her maid and was now her housekeeper. The entire school fizzed with anticipation, and it was hard not to feel left out. Flora had had four postcards and a long letter from the other Flora's mother, but of course it wasn't the same.

"The two years will pass sooner than you think," Mother had written, *"before you even know it. And I'll be thinking about you, every single minute of every single day. When we love each other so much, nothing can really keep us apart."*

"Flora, are you all right?" Virginia Denning gently touched her arm.

"Sorry, I was thinking about – about—" Flora pushed away the memory of the other Flora. "I was miles away."

"I was just saying, don't be too downcast about staying at school for half-term. Quite a few of us do, and we have plenty of fun. Last year Cook let us make toffee, and we all crammed into Bradley's study to listen to the wireless. It was a hoot."

They were having tea, and all the other girls round the long table seemed to be chattering about their parents. This must be what had thrown her into the other Flora's mind. She was getting good at fighting off the other Flora, but there were still these eerie moments of being inside her feelings.

She had eaten her white bread and butter, and was now chewing through a slab of the fruit cake from her tuck box. Virginia, sitting beside her, was eating tiny, elegant biscuits with pink icing.

She pushed her plate towards Flora. "Do have one. Mother sends them from Vienna."

"Thanks." Flora took a biscuit. It melted deliciously on her tongue. "Oh, that's wicked – I mean, it's lovely! Is Vienna where you come from?"

"My mother was born there," Virginia said. "She's a Frozel."

"A – what?"

"Frozel's is a very well-known department store."

"Oh, you mean like Harrods, or something?"

Virginia laughed, which made her look younger and much prettier. "Yes, rather like Harrods. You do have the most priceless way of talking – I'm almost sorry you're starting to lose that accent. I think it's charming. Have another wicked biscuit."

"Thanks." Flora found she didn't mind when Virginia teased her about her modern accent, she did it so kindly. "You don't sound at all foreign."

"My father's English, and I mostly grew up in Paris, where he was a professor at the university. I came here when they went to live in Vienna, because my governess got married and none of the Viennese schools would have me."

"Why not? Did you fail all the exams?"

"They don't admit Jews," Virginia said. "Not the schools my people liked, at any rate."

"But – just because you're Jewish? That's disgusting!"

Virginia was amused by her indignation. "To be fair, a couple of the schools were run by nuns – just

137

imagine, I might have ended up in a convent. I'm jolly glad I ended up at St Win's. I say, may I have the rest of your cake? My mother thinks English fruit cake is an abomination, but I adore it."

"Go ahead." Flora was uneasy, and didn't know why. It was something to do with the Second World War — if only she'd paid more attention in Ms Stuart's lessons, but it wasn't only that — her brain was marbled with someone else's memories, and it refused to tell her why she was afraid.

On the morning of half-term — a bright, gusty, spring-like morning — the entrance hall of the school was a scene of chaos. Girls, teachers and parents milled around the hall, the stairs and the drive outside.

Flora and Pete gazed down on the crowd from the top of the stairs. Flora thought she had never seen so many hats.

"Are you sure this is all right?" she asked again. She had been invited to spend the day with Pete and her parents.

"Of course — I wrote to tell them you were coming. They like me to bring friends. You mustn't be shy. They're harmless old things." She grabbed the sleeve of Flora's blouse and tugged her down the stairs. "Crikey, that must be Pogo's brother!"

A noisy motorbike, with a sidecar, came roaring up

to the bottom of the front steps.

"Nev!" shrieked Pogo, shooting out of the crowd like a cork from a champagne bottle.

The motorbike spluttered to a halt and Neville dismounted. He was wearing a long, flapping leather coat and a kind of leather helmet. "Pogo, old bean!"

The two of them laughed and slapped each other on the back, and Flora decided she liked Neville. He was small and thin, just like Pogo. He had untidy brown hair, big round glasses, and a face that was even more monkey-like than his sister's – but with a turned-up nose that made it particularly funny and nice.

Pogo proudly introduced him to her friends. "Nev, please meet Flora, Pete and Dulcie – the gang from the dorm."

"She's written me loads about you all," Neville said cheerfully. "I know exactly who you are. You're Flora, the girl from India – you're Dulcie the cherub – and that means you're She Who Must Be Obeyed, also known as Pete."

This made them all laugh so much that nobody noticed the headmistress coming towards them, looking severely at Neville. "Who is this young man?"

Pogo turned bright red and blurted out, "This is my brother, Miss Powers-Prout!"

To Flora's surprise, the old dragon nearly smiled when she shook hands with Neville. "Mr Lawrence, you're surely not taking Cecilia in that contraption?"

"What, the bike? It's safe as houses! Don't worry, Miss Powers-Prout – I promise I'll bring her back in one piece!"

He climbed back on to the saddle, Pogo climbed into the very flimsy-looking sidecar, and the motorbike roared away down the drive. *Lucky her*, Flora thought. *She gets a day of freedom, without spooky 1930s grown-ups. I so hope Pete's parents are OK.*

There were dozens of cars in the drive now, and dozens of people milling about. The cars were large and boxy, with running boards and big headlamps. Flora watched the headmistress moving in stately fashion, greeting parents. She watched Dulcie hugging a stout old lady so like her that she had to be her grandmother. She had come with another old lady, who was thin and rigid, and wearing a hat like a varnished flowerpot.

"That must be Dorsey," Flora said, "the one who makes the fudge."

Pete was no longer beside her. Flora saw her crashing impatiently through the crowd, and flinging herself at a man and woman with grey hair.

Flora felt very lonely, standing here with nobody to claim her – like the last piece of luggage on the carousel at the airport. But Pete did not forget her for long. She dashed over and grabbed her hand.

"Come on – come and meet my people – I'm just

140

giving them their instructions."

Mr Peterson was tall and thin, with a grey moustache. His wife was shorter – hardly taller than Pete – with a plump, kind face under a neat felt hat.

"This is Flora, and we know exactly what we want to do today: lunch in a café, you know, with choices; then the old castle, then a slap-up tea with poached eggs on toast—"

"Daphne, do calm down," Mrs Peterson said. "You know we'll do exactly as you say, dear – don't we always? I'm very glad to meet you, Flora. It's so nice to meet Daphne's friends."

"Mummy! Stop calling me Daphne!"

"No, dear," Mrs Peterson said calmly, "that is one command I will not obey. It's a beautiful name."

"It's a stupid name."

"Now then," said Pete's father. He smiled down at Flora as he shook her hand. "How do you do, Flora?"

He was a lot like Pete, with his thin face, rather beaky nose and brilliant blue eyes. The corners of his eyes wrinkled up, and Flora drew in her breath sharply – for a moment, he looked just like her dad.

"Hold your horses, old lady," he told Pete. "Your mother wants to speak to the head before we shoot off."

Flora swallowed hard. There was a lump in her throat and she had to fight back the tears. Mr Peterson didn't really look that much like Dad – but the reminder suddenly made her miss her parents so much that it hurt.

She managed not to break down until the Petersons had joined the group of people around Miss Powers-Prout, then she ducked away into the box room, where the tuck boxes were kept, to cry in private. It was dark and damp, and smelled of mouldy jam. Flora sat down on the stone floor, took her cotton hanky from the leg of her knickers (there were no tissues in the 1930s), and let out a storm of sobs.

The door opened. *Pete's come looking for me*, she thought hopefully.

It was Consuela Carver.

She slowly walked towards Flora, and stood staring down at her blankly. Flora went on crying, too miserable to care what the Carver thought of her.

"You're crying," Consuela said. "I expect you're crying because your mother and father aren't here."

"Yes," Flora said.

Consuela leaned against a shelf of tuck boxes. "Mine aren't here either."

Flora had not expected this. "Oh."

"My father's in Kenya. My mother's only in London, but she doesn't like coming to school things."

"Oh."

"They're divorced. I bet you've never met anyone

142

whose parents are divorced."

Flora blew her nose. "Course I have – my best friend—" She stopped. Ella was no longer her best friend, and she was far away in the future.

"I suppose you'll tell Pete," Consuela said bitterly. "And now she'll rag me about it."

It was incredible, but Flora felt sorry for her. Consuela had taken off her sneering mask, and the face underneath was only sad.

"I won't tell," she said. "I won't tell anyone. But you shouldn't feel bad about it – it's not your fault."

There was a silence. Flora couldn't tell what Consuela was thinking.

In her normal voice, she said, "I'm going out with the Elliots. Are you going out with someone?"

"The Petersons."

"Have a nice time." Consuela – her face blank again – walked out of the room.

Flora mopped her face, thinking about this strange encounter. At APS at least half the class had divorced parents, and it was no big deal – certainly not something to be ashamed of. Suddenly, it wasn't so easy to hate Consuela. It was one thing to have parents who were lost in time or far away in India, but how must it feel to have a mother who hadn't come because she didn't care enough?

*

The Petersons' car took them along narrow country roads. The 1930s countryside was untidier than the countryside of the twenty-firt century, but also prettier. The fields were smaller than the fields you saw beside the motorways of the future, and divided by big, shaggy hedges studded with spring flowers. There were no electricity pylons, no overhead wires, and hardly any other cars. They had to slow down several times, behind wagons drawn by horses.

Pete was in radiant high spirits, talking nineteen to the dozen and rapping out orders. Flora was a little shocked by the way Mr and Mrs Peterson kept giving in to her. Uneasily, she wondered if this was how she sounded when she spoke to her own parents. Yes, she often told Mum and Dad what to do. They liked to be told, because they wanted her to be happy. But she hoped she wasn't as bossy as Pete.

They stopped for lunch at a hotel in a small country town. Pete fussed over the menu for ages, and told her parents what food to order, so that she could have a taste of it. "If you send me to a school where the food's putrid, the least you can do is let me eat what I like when I have a day off. Flora, you have the roast lamb. Mummy, you can have the liver and bacon . . ."

After lunch, they went to see the ruins of an old castle, and Flora and Pete had a fine time climbing over the stones. When they were tired, Mrs Peterson took a

Thermos flask from her basket, and they all had a cup of tea. Mr Peterson smoked a pipe. Flora looked at him as hard as she could, without staring rudely. Was he really like her own dad, or did she see it because she missed him so much?

Pete's mother asked a lot of questions about her family, and Flora had to concentrate on giving the right answers from the life of the other Flora.

"We know some Foxes," Mrs Peterson said. "We met them at Sheringham, a few summers ago. Daphne, do you remember?"

"Nope."

"Don't say 'nope', dear, this isn't a cowboy film. They had that little boy you were always squabbling with."

Pete rolled her eyes. "Why do you always want to talk about such dull things? I'm starving again. Aren't you worried that I'm so hungry all the time?"

"You're a growing girl," Mr Peterson said comfortably.

"I mean, doesn't it speak volumes about the quality of the food at that place? And there's never enough of it, is there, Flora? I think you should write to Old Peepy about it."

Her father said, "Never mind, we'll get you another box of chocs for the tuck box."

"Thanks, Daddy – it's looking jolly empty and it's got to last me till the end of term."

Her mother laughed, and lovingly smoothed Pete's untidy hair. "I'll throw in a tin of biscuits, but that's all you're getting."

Flora didn't believe this for a moment. These two made her own doting parents look strict. They treated their daughter like a goddess; no wonder she always expected to be in charge. A scary thought came to her that perhaps she didn't like Pete very much.

But she did like Pete. It was impossible not to, when she was lively and brilliant and funny, and blew into a room like fresh air. Today, she was a beacon of happiness, and she generously included Flora in every treat. The two of them returned to school at bedtime exhausted, and blissfully stuffed with stodgy 1930s food.

When they all lay in bed after lights out, comparing notes in yawny whispers, it turned out that Dulcie had also spent most of the day eating.

"Dorsey's friend has a tea shop, and we had cream horns, coffee éclairs, the loveliest little sandwiches—"

"I'm amazed you didn't all explode," Pogo whispered. "Neville and I were heaps too busy to waste time with unproductive guzzling – though we did have some very decent fish and chips. He let me drive the bike when the roads were quiet. And we had a lot of talking to do, because we like to set the world to rights. I asked Nev about your war, Flora, and he says it's perfectly possible. I did so wish I could tell him you were from the future!"

Where was she from? On the edge of falling asleep, Flora hardly knew. Did Pete's dad remind her of her real dad, or Colonel Fox from Poona? And which one of them did she remember talking about Sheringham? The trouble with two lots of memories was that your brain tied itself in knots.

13

Measles

A few days after half-term, there came a morning when Dulcie and Pogo could not get out of bed. They shivered and moaned, and Dulcie said plaintively, "I hurt in every single bit of me!"

Pogo muttered, "Go AWAY!" and buried her head in the bedclothes.

"This is serious," Pete said. "We'd better fetch Matron."

Flora, the first to be dressed, ran upstairs to the sanatorium.

"Don't tell me!" sighed Matron. "It never rains but it pours." She clamped a hand across Flora's forehead. "Have you had measles, dear?"

Flora nearly said she'd had the MMR injection when

she was a baby, but remembered it hadn't been invented yet, and dipped hastily into the memories of the other Flora. "Yes, Matron, when I was four."

"Good girl, you're one less to worry about. Now, let's have a look at your chums."

Matron came back to the bedroom with Flora, and there was something very comforting about her short, round, starchy presence.

Kind and brisk, she felt the foreheads of Pogo and Dulcie. "Yes, it's measles, all right – you're as hot as a pair of little furnaces! We'll put you both to bed in the san, and you'll feel ever so much better when the spots come out. Dear me, we haven't had an outbreak like this for years. Daphne, you've had measles, haven't you?"

"Yes, Matron. I'm as fit as a fiddle."

"In that case, dear, shouldn't you get dressed? Or do you plan to go down to breakfast like that?"

Pete suddenly realized that she was in her vest and knickers, and her squeak of alarm was so funny that even Dulcie giggled weakly.

"Measles is beastly," Pete told Flora, once she had flung on the rest of her clothes, and the two of them were hurrying downstairs. "I had it when I was six. Daddy bought me a doll's house – but I'd rather not have had the measles in the first place. You come out in bright red spots."

"Gross!" Flora said, feeling very sorry for Dulcie and Pogo.

They were late for breakfast, but nobody took any notice. Their long table was emptier than usual, and Flora tried to work out who was missing.

"Jill's got it," Bunty Hardwick told them. "And Peggy Waterman, and both the Scarborough twins. And Virginia Denning – which is jolly bad luck on her, because she's seventeen, and it's worse when you're old."

"And I don't see Consuela Carver," Pete said cheerfully. "How sad, to think of that perfect face ruined by hideous spots!"

"My big brother had measles frightfully badly," someone piped up. "He had to wear blue glasses and stay off school for a whole term. It can make you blind and deaf, and all sorts of things."

Bunty said, "One of my aunts died of it."

"Well, the teachers all seem to be in rude health, worse luck," said Pete. "I was hoping we'd get some time off lessons."

Flora couldn't take it so lightly. Mum had told her how dangerous measles could be. She'd told her that Roald Dahl – the man who wrote *Charlie and the Chocolate Factory* – had had a little daughter who died of measles. The idea of Dulcie or Pogo dying was too terrifying to think about.

The school was in a state of emergency. In assembly, Miss Powers-Prout announced that eleven girls were ill, and said a prayer for them. The healthy girls were told to wear their bedroom slippers, keep the school as quiet as possible, and tell someone immediately if they felt ill because measles was highly infectious.

The next three days were hushed and serious. They spoke in soft voices and crept about in their slippers. The teachers taught lessons in their slippers, and it wasn't even funny. Three professional nurses arrived. The local doctor, a youngish man in a brown tweed suit, came twice a day. A very important doctor arrived, with a black coat and pointed grey beard, and a whisper went round that he was a "specialist" who had come to see Virginia.

People's parents began to appear. The girls watched them being led through the hall, anxious and flustered, carrying flowers and bunches of grapes. Dulcie's granny came, with such a heavy basket of treats that Ethel had to help her carry it up to the san. Neville came on his motorbike, with a pile of books and comics for Pogo.

Virginia's parents were in Vienna, but a cousin came to see her. This cousin was a young woman rumoured to be a real actress on the London stage, and her glamorous appearance created a sensation – the entire lower school lined the windows to stare at her. She wore lipstick and furs, and left behind her a delicious smell of perfume. Flora thought her dark hair was weird and shiny and looked like a wig, but Pete said shut up, it was divine.

Consuela's mother created another sensation, by sending a tower of pink hot-house roses, as tall as a person. It stood in the hall in a white basket tied with pink ribbon, and the girls clustered round it, sighing with awe and admiration.

"She didn't come herself, though," Flora said. "Consuela's the only one who hasn't had a visitor."

"She's too nasty to visit," said Pete. "Don't tell me you're sorry for her!"

Flora didn't say any more because boredom was making Pete argumentative, and she didn't want to argue. But she was sorry for the Carver. She couldn't help remembering the odd, stilted conversation they'd had in the box room. In that second, she had seen Consuela's sadness, and she couldn't get it out of her mind.

On the fifth day, Matron said the infectious stage was over, and Pete and Flora could visit their friends.

"But please remember that this is a sickroom and not a bear garden. You may stay for exactly ten minutes, and I don't want to hear any loud voices."

They found Dulcie and Pogo in a small, bare, white-painted room on the top floor, both a little weak and groggy but (to Flora's great relief) obviously not dying.

"Keep the curtains closed," Matron said, on her way out. "I know it's gloomy, but they mustn't strain their eyes. Measles can leave the eyes very weak."

"You can't imagine how bored we are!" Pogo sighed. "I could just about bear it if we were allowed to read – but Matron says we have to rest our eyes for a whole week. If Bradley didn't read to us, I think I'd throw myself out of the window."

"We're not allowed to eat anything but mush," Dulcie told them solemnly. "I didn't care at first, because I wasn't hungry. But I'm jolly hungry today, and all I can think about is the Chelsea buns Granny brought me. You two are so lucky to be well!"

"That's what you think," Pete said. "As a matter of fact, all us healthy types are having a pretty hard time – aren't we, Flora? For one thing, the food's horrid because the kitchens are too busy making grub for you precious little invalids. And we're not allowed to make the smallest noise. It's actually frightful."

"Poor you," Pogo said, "how you've suffered."

This made Flora laugh. She strongly suspected that Pete was jealous of the sick girls for hogging all the attention, and she was getting tired of her self-centred complaints. "Don't listen to her," she told Pogo. "It's not that bad. We're supposed to be cheering you up."

Pete wandered over to the window, to peep through the crack in the curtains. "You both look cheerful enough, I must say. And why wouldn't you be? You lie in bed all day and you don't have any lessons."

Flora and Pogo rolled their eyes at each other, and smiled. Flora had missed Pogo's wry sending-up of Pete. She asked, "Are you really feeling better?"

"Oh, yes," Pogo said. "I think we got off lightly. Poor old Virginia's still pretty seedy, but the rest of us are over the worst now."

"I felt heaps better the minute I smelled the buns," said Dulcie. "It's so incredibly mean that I'm not allowed to eat one."

Flora was anxious. "Was Virginia very ill?"

"Yes," Pogo said. "Matron had to sit up all night with her, and they were all set to send a telegram to summon her parents – but don't worry, I heard one of the nurses saying she'd turned the corner."

"Poor thing!" Flora liked Virginia, and was glad she was recovering.

"You two are absolutely covered with spots," Pete observed. "I've only just noticed because it's so dark in here. Are they just on your faces, or all over?"

"That's quite enough, young lady." Matron came back into the room in time to hear this. "I'm sure you had spots in all kinds of places when you had the measles. Now, it's time you left Cecilia and Dulcie to rest."

"But I don't need any more rest!" groaned Pogo. "Please, Matron – couldn't we have just five more minutes?"

"Not today, dear. If you're feeling better tomorrow, they can stay for a whole half-hour."

"Couldn't I read something? Anything?"

Matron smiled, and tucked in Pogo's bedclothes. "What a one you are for your books! But I'm afraid you really do need to rest your eyes, dear – you'll thank me for it one day."

"We'll read to you tomorrow," Flora said, feeling sorry for her – poor old Pogo was a book addict, and she must be in agony. "Won't we, Pete?"

"I s'pose," Pete said grudgingly. "As long as it's not something too dull, or in Latin."

"That's very thoughtful of you, Flora." Matron's round face beamed approval. "I must say, you and Daphne have perked up my invalids no end. You can come again tomorrow, at the same time."

And that was that, because not even teachers dared to argue with Matron. In her sanatorium she ruled with a rod of iron, and her patients were forced to live like invalids long after they started feeling better. At home in the future, people weren't allowed to be ill for more than a couple of days. When Dad was getting over pneumonia, the doctors and nurses had nagged him to "keep moving". In the past, they had to behave as if they were made of glass.

As the days passed, Pete and Flora fell into a routine of visiting their friends every afternoon. Matron was now making them sit up in a long room with a glass roof. In dressing gowns and slippers they played board games and stared out of the window at the rainy countryside, until it was time to eat mushy food and go back to bed. Pogo said she was so desperately bored, she knew the fire-drill instructions pinned to the wall off by heart. Flora tried to read to her, but the sun room was too noisy – at visiting hour it was packed. Everyone's friends looked in, including (to Pete's annoyance) the Carver's gang of cronies.

Consuela was still Pete's foe, and Pete still had to put up with her mean remarks. But she stopped picking on Flora. It wasn't that she was nice to her. She had simply decided not to notice Flora any more. When Flora and Pete visited their friends in the sun room, they had to walk past Consuela – glamorous, despite her spots, in a pink satin dressing gown sent by her mother – but Pete was the only victim of the Carver tongue.

"Oh, look – a scarecrow! How did it get out of the kitchen garden? Goodness, it's Pete – her poor family can't even afford a comb!"

By the time the state of emergency had lasted a fortnight, Pete was seething with frustration. "I could get back at her, if it wasn't for Matron breathing down my neck."

"Oh, Pete, can't you just forget about Consuela?"

"WHAT is all this being sweetness and light to the Carver? Why do you care about her?"

Flora sighed. "I don't like her any more than you do. It's getting boring, that's all."

"Oh, I DO beg your pardon!" Pete furiously charged ahead of her into the sanatorium's sun room, almost banging the swing door in Flora's face. "But I refuse to be nice to her – even her own mother keeps away from her!"

Consuela, in her armchair near the door, raised her head sharply. Had she heard? Her pretty face was a cold mask.

"I don't believe you sometimes," Flora hissed at Pete. "That was really mean!"

"Oh, go away, Goody Two-Shoes!" snapped Pete. "You're just being a coward because she's been ill. It hasn't turned her into a saint, you know. You get punished for NOT being ill in this school. The ill girls have all the nice things!"

Pogo and Dulcie, waiting at their table, heard the end of this.

"Greetings, healthy animals," Pogo said, grinning. "You're about to get your fair share of something very nice indeed. You tell them, Dulcie."

For the first time since measles, Dulcie's cheeks were pink. "It's dreadfully exciting: Old Peepy's shutting the school, because it's being – what was the word?"

"Fumigated," Pogo said. "To remove the germs."

"Yes, and that means the Easter hols will be three whole weeks – and Granny's invited you all to spend them with us! Oh, I can't WAIT to show you everything!"

Pete and Flora, their argument forgotten, stared at each other. This sounded too good to be true. Dulcie's granny – Lady Badger – lived in a big old farmhouse beside the sea, and Dulcie described it as a paradise of delicious food and adorable animals.

Pogo said, "Isn't it ripping? My brothers and I usually spend our holidays in Birmingham, with our uncle and aunt. It's very nice and all that – and I'll certainly miss seeing my dear old brothers this hols – but it's almost worth having measles for three whole weeks by the sea. It's awfully decent of Lady Badger, Dulcie."

Dulcie and Pogo were still in the san these days, though they wore school uniform and came downstairs for meals. Dulcie's cheeks had lost their roundness, and her legs were long and spidery, as if they had stretched. Skinny Pogo was a little skeleton.

"The doctor says sea air is important after measles," Dulcie said. "And that makes our house perfect. Virginia's coming too."

"Good for her – the more the merrier!" Pete's bad mood had melted away. "Won't it be spiffing?"

158

Pete and Flora passed Virginia's room on their way downstairs, and the door was open. Flora looked inside.

Virginia sat in an armchair beside the window, with an eiderdown over her knees. She was very thin and white-faced, but she smiled when she saw the two girls.

"Hello, Flora – hello, Pete. Do come in."

They both took a few steps into the room.

Flora asked, "How are you?"

"Fine , thank you – well enough to be bored."

"We heard about you coming to Dulcie's," Pete said.

Virginia smiled. "It's a lark, isn't it? I was petrified my mother would make me come home to Vienna – she wants me to leave St Win's and go to a finishing school. But my good old dad says he'd like me to have the benefit of sea air, and that means I'm safe for another term."

"Don't!" Flora said.

Pete and Virginia looked at her.

Virginia asked, "Don't what?"

"Oh – nothing." Flora wanted to say, "Don't go back to Vienna." But it sounded stupid when Virginia wasn't allowed to know why.

14

Merrythorpe

"It's a case of all hands to the pump," Miss Bradley said cheerfully. "We can't spare a teacher, so Virginia's your official escort – and you'd better behave like saints."

St Winifred's had closed for fumigation, and both the narrow platforms of the little country station were crowded with excited girls. Watkins, the stationmaster, had taken on a couple of extra men to help with the mountains of luggage.

"I don't think they'll give me much trouble," Virginia said, smiling.

Flora felt a little shy with Virginia today. She was not wearing her school uniform but a proper grown-up dress and coat, and even lipstick. Her unflattering glasses had gone, and she had taken trouble with her hair. She seemed very old and distant – until she suddenly whispered to Flora, "Is the lipstick idiotic? I'm trying to look as if I'm in charge."

"It looks really nice," Flora whispered back. She was glad they were travelling down to Merrythorpe (the name of Dulcie's house) with Virginia instead of a teacher. It made this feel like a real holiday. Spring had come, the air smelled of soil and blossom, the trees and hedgerows were covered with green buds, and the sun shone from a cloudless sky.

The train came, puffing out cushions of steam like a train in a film about the olden days.

Pete was so excited that she dropped her overnight bag, showering the platform with pyjamas, books, sponge bag and loose sweets. There was a moment of chaos when she bent down to pick everything up and Dulcie fell over her. Somehow, they all managed to gather Pete's belongings and climb into the train. The five of them had a compartment to themselves.

"We're moving!" crowed Pete. "I'm so wild with happiness, I feel I could fly! No more lessons for three whole weeks!"

"Let's have some fudge," Dulcie said, pulling a paper bag from her pocket.

"Crikey, we've just had breakfast," said Flora (the word "crikey" came quite easily to her these days). "Oh, go on then – if only it wasn't so delicious."

"No, thanks," Virginia said. "I'm not up to the effort of eating fudge." Once you looked past the lipstick, she was very pale and there were grey smudges under her eyes.

Pete blurted out, "I say, you are better, aren't you? Peggy Waterman told me you nearly died."

"That's a bit of an exaggeration," Virginia said. "But I was laid rather low. Matron was almost cross with me for getting so ill. She kept saying she couldn't imagine how I'd reached the age of seventeen without being exposed to measles. I suppose it's because I've spent most of my time with grown-ups, and didn't mix much with other children."

Flora, as the only child of ancient parents, was interested. "Were you lonely?"

"Not at all. I liked being one of the adults. But my father didn't like it. He said that before my mother launched me into society, I needed to learn how to be a real girl."

"But you are a real girl! What did you need to learn?"

"Just about everything – how to take a joke, how to make friends, how to share things. I was furious at first, but now I see that he was right. Before I came to St Win's, I was a pampered little madam and I thought I was at the centre of the universe."

"You're not like that now." Uneasily, Flora wondered

162

if she had been a "pampered little madam" herself, and had to push away certain embarrassing memories of the way she had treated Mum and Dad.

"I had my corners rubbed off," Virginia said. "It wasn't painful." She leaned back against the seat. "My dear Dulcie, how can you possibly have finished all that fudge?"

"I can't help it," Dulcie said, with her mouth full. "I'm so ravenously hungry – it's as if there's a nest of baby birds inside me with their beaks open. D'you think it's too early to have our sandwiches?" Dulcie had lost most of her plumpness, and seemed to have grown about six inches, until she was all eyes and legs and plaits. She looked wistfully at the big, moist parcel of sandwiches they had been given for their lunch. It was half past ten.

"Let's open them now." Pogo was similarly skinny and ravenous. "There isn't anyone here to stop us – unless Virginia says we can't."

"Good gracious, don't mind me," Virginia said. "I'm far too feeble to exercise any kind of authority."

Pogo unwrapped the sandwiches. They were filled with egg and cress, and Pete groaned.

"Do you have to? They smell of Number Twos!"

That was all it took to make them shriek with laughter. Flora wondered how long it was since she had laughed as hard as this. She remembered another spring day, last year, in Ella's back garden, when Ella's dog had suddenly snatched a chocolate muffin out of her hand, and they had rolled about on the lawn absolutely screaming. It was odd, she thought – the more she liked Pete, Pogo and Dulcie, the more she found herself missing Ella. There were so many things she wanted to say to her. She had a feeling Ella would have got on well at St Winifred's. She liked serious things, like reading and writing and talking about history, and when they were on the awful holiday in Italy, she had loved listening to Granny's stories about her famous artist lover.

Flora was beginning to revise her opinion of Granny. She didn't like her any better, but you had to admit she'd had an interesting life. Pogo, Dulcie and Pete (especially Pete) couldn't hear enough about the wild parties and the four husbands. Deep down, Flora was rather proud of her, and sorry she had spent most of the Italian holiday sulking because there wasn't a pool.

At Plymouth, they changed to a funny little train with crates of chickens in the guard's van. It chugged across the countryside, through a beautiful landscape of woods and hills and deep, sheltered valleys. They passed fields where the ploughs were pulled by horses, and stopped for ages in tiny, silent stations.

Dulcie was getting more and more excited, and Flora envied her. She was going to see her home, and the people she loved. No wonder she was pale and almost trembling with impatience. Flora had one of her intense moments of longing for home. The deeper they went into the 1930s countryside, the further they seemed to be from her real life.

Dulcie's local station was called Cranton Halt, and it was not much more than a small platform and a stationmaster's hut. The girls stepped out of the train into the sharp spring afternoon.

"Granny!" cried Dulcie. She ran along the platform on her new spidery legs, and fell into the arms of her grandmother.

Flora remembered Lady Badger from half-term, and she looked so much like an elderly Dulcie that Flora could have picked her out of a crowd. Her yellow hair had turned white, and her round cheeks had sagged, but her blue eyes had the same expression of innocence. And when she held out her hand to the girls, she gave them a very Dulcie-ish smile.

"My dears, I'm so very glad to see you all – you must be dreadfully tired, but we're only ten minutes away from Merrythorpe, and I hope you're all hungry – Dorsey's been cooking herself into a frenzy." She looked at Virginia. "Poor child, you're ready to drop. Come and sit in the front of the car, and the little girls can go in the back. And don't fret about the luggage," she added. "Mr Rudge says he'll bring it as soon as the express has gone through."

A large, black, boxy car waited on the patch of gravel outside the miniature station. Flora, Pete, Dulcie and Pogo crammed on to the slippery leather seat in the back. There were no seat belts – 1930s people didn't seem to worry about danger as much as people in the twenty-first century.

Lady Badger drove very slowly and very carefully, goggling earnestly at the road like Dulcie on the hockey field. She inched the car down twisting, narrow lanes, through woods with patches of daffodils, and past banks of primroses.

"This is the prettiest place I've ever seen," Pete said. "Wake up, Pogo – you'll miss the first sight of the sea!"

Pogo was very tired, but she forced her eyes open. None of them could bear to miss a thing.

At last, between clumps of trees, they glimpsed the sea, shining like a sheet of steel in the last of the clear spring light. They all cheered.

Dulcie bounced with happiness and greeted familiar landmarks as if she had been away for a hundred years. "There's the mill – and the church – oh, it all looks ripping! What's the news, Granny? You haven't told me a thing!"

"Well, dear," Lady Badger said, "it's been one excitement after another. Tara had a nice little bull calf, and Mr Knight says you're welcome to visit. And

Dr Thompson's horse threw him into a ditch – he was perfectly all right, only bruised. And there was a fire at the post office. Mrs Cooper's son put it out, but not before the entire stock of knitting wool was ruined. The rain has been frightful, but the barometer says 'set fair' and I think it's going to be lovely – though Dorsey doesn't agree – you know how she never agrees with the barometer."

"We're here!" squeaked Dulcie.

The car turned a corner, and slowed beside a pair of stone gateposts. "Carefully does it," said Lady Badger, violently changing gear. "I can't count the times I've bumped into these posts! Welcome to Merrythorpe, my dears."

"Oh, how WIZARD!" gasped Pete.

And it really was gorgeous. Flora had been worried that someone called "Lady" would live in a stately home. This was a long, low, friendly-looking house of soft grey stone, with gardens that swept down to the top of the cliff. The girls got out of the car. Flora smelled the sea air, and heard the waves, and the seagulls, and knew this holiday was going to be wonderful.

Dulcie ran to hug the rigid, dark figure waiting on the front steps. "Dorsey!"

Dorsey was old and stern. Her dark grey hair was scraped back into a hard knot and looked as if it had been painted on. She did not bend when Dulcie kissed her, but stared at her with intense disapproval.

"Look at you, you're skin and bone! You haven't come home a minute too soon — you'll sit right down and have some decent food."

The hall of Merrythorpe smelled of wood fires, lavender soap, furniture polish, sponge cake, and a hundred other nice things that Flora couldn't identify. Two large yellow dogs ran in, and Dulcie dropped to her knees to cover their furry faces with kisses.

"Their names are Paul and Silas," Lady Badger said, "after the apostles who were in prison, because they were born at the police station. Do get up, darling — it can't be wise to kiss dogs when you're getting over measles. Take your friends to wash their hands for tea."

They took turns in the downstairs cloakroom at the end of a long passage.

"Isn't this topping?" sighed Pete, rinsing her hands in a tempest of splashes. "Do you think Lady B. will let us run outside after tea? Do you think it'll be too late to go to the beach? I'm sorry not to be seeing my people this hols — but this is heaps nicer than dull old London." She was electric with happiness. In this mood Pete was great, and Flora couldn't remember why she had ever not liked her.

A superb tea waited for them on the big kitchen table. There were plates of cakes, sandwiches and buns, and Dorsey had made them each a cup of hot chocolate and a boiled egg. She sternly made sure they all ate until they were stuffed, and Flora was surprised by her own appetite – how putrid it would be if she suddenly returned home and found she'd got so fat that none of her clothes fitted any more – but she was very hungry, and the food was fantastic.

Dorsey was especially strict with Virginia. She pushed her into an armchair, threw a blanket over her knees and said, "You're the biggest disgrace of the lot, young lady – you haven't touched your egg!"

"I'm sorry, Dorsey," Virginia said meekly.

"I'll fetch you a nice basin of broth."

"Oh – I don't think I could—"

"Nonsense!"

"You'd better listen to Dorsey, dear," said Lady Badger. "Everybody in this house listens to Dorsey."

"That's because I'm the only one with any sense," Dorsey said. "Stop feeding that dog, Madam – I can see you!"

Lady Badger had been passing bits of cake under the table to one of the Labradors. She giggled and turned pink, and Flora suddenly realized that this was what Dulcie would look like when she was an old lady in the twenty-first century – a very weird thought.

The four younger girls were to sleep in the old nursery, which was now Dulcie's bedroom. It was a long room with a low ceiling, and a wide window looking out over the sea. There were shelves of old toys and books, and a framed picture of a man in armour crouching at the feet of a ragged girl – *King Cophetua and the Beggar-maid*, Flora remembered. There was also a large photograph of Dulcie's dead parents on their wedding day. Three more beds had been brought in. One was a camp bed.

"Bags I!" yelled Pete, flinging herself down on it and making it creak alarmingly. "Dulcie, I think you live in heaven!"

Dulcie beamed proudly. "Isn't it fun that we're all together? It's as if our school bedroom had flown away to another house."

"Where's Virginia?" asked Flora.

"In the spare room, next to Granny. She's too nearly grown up to sleep in here."

When she first arrived at St Winifred's, Flora would have envied Virginia for having a room to herself.

How I've changed, she thought. *Now I'd much rather be in here with my friends.*

They left the curtains open, to gaze at the view while they put on their pyjamas. Night had fallen, and the horizon slowly disappeared in an inky wash of darkness.

After Dulcie had switched off the lamp, Flora lay on her back in the soft bed, looking drowsily at the beams in the ceiling and listening to the sound of the waves. Pete, on the camp bed beside her, had fallen asleep — after dancing the cancan in her knickers, until they all nearly died of laughing.

I'll miss her when I go home, Flora thought.

The time was coming. She felt it coming. Any day might be the day she discovered what she had been sent here to do.

15

One Last Spell

The morning was glorious – it was incredibly exciting to wake up to blue sky and sunlit sea. The four younger girls could hardly wait to finish their breakfasts and run out to the beach. Virginia said she was tired and would stay in the house, but Flora, Pete and Pogo couldn't wait to start exploring. At last, when Dorsey decided they had eaten enough, they were free. Flora's parents always took their holidays abroad, in places where the beaches were flat and white and hot, and she had never explored the British seaside.

There were no deckchairs on this beach, or shops, or cafés. It was simply a small patch of pale sand, surrounded by piles of rocks that were bearded with clumps of seaweed. Dressed in her comfortable games clothes, Flora climbed the slippery rocks and paddled in the boisterous, freezing sea. Here was another example of how she'd changed – the old Flora might have wanted cappuccino and high-factor suncream, and yearned to bask like a lizard in searing heat. The new Flora loved the climbing and the messing about in rock pools. She had never felt so adventurous, or so free.

Dulcie's granny thought they should run around outdoors from dawn to dusk, without being bothered by grown-ups, and it was the first time Flora had ever climbed anything higher than a flight of stairs without someone shouting, "Be careful!" On their second day, Lady Badger announced that she had borrowed three extra bicycles, and they could all go cycling. Flora could ride a bike, but not very well, and her first, wobbling efforts made the others giggle.

"My parents don't let me ride on the roads," Flora explained, "because there's just too much traffic in the twenty-first century. Are you sure we're allowed?"

"Gosh, of course we're allowed!" Pete said. "Where else would you ride a bike?"

"Well, I don't know . . ." Flora looked doubtfully at the bike she had been lent. At home, the pale green bike she sometimes rode in the park was as light as a feather, bristling with gears, bells and reflector strips. This old monster had a very heavy dark blue frame

173

and no gears. There was a big, square wicker basket between the handlebars. Stopping and starting were much more of an effort. But she didn't want the others to see that she was nervous.

The roads around Merrythorpe were narrow and winding, with absolutely no traffic except the occasional tractor or farm cart. Flora did her best to keep up with the others, and quickly gained enough confidence to love the sensation of shooting along the grey ribbons of road with the wind in her face. Once you got used to the differences, they didn't seem to matter. She was soon jumping on and off almost as nimbly as Pete.

As the days passed, they explored up and down the coast, and all the nearby villages. Dorsey sent them off every morning with a huge packed lunch, and they picnicked whenever they felt like stopping – usually fairly soon after they had set out, owing to the ferocious appetites of Dulcie and Pogo. They cycled for miles, and by the time they returned to Merrythorpe for tea (Dorsey was always looking out for them, and always accusing them of being late), they were bone-tired and ravenously hungry.

Flora spent her days in the open air, being battered by the winds, baked by the sun and scoured with salt and sand. In the evenings she was too exhausted to do more than lie on the rug beside the fire, with her arm round one of the dogs, while Lady Badger read the *Just-So Stories* aloud. Sometimes, she wondered about the other Flora. If she was staying on for an extra term at St Winifred's, the other Flora must be staying on at Penrice Hall. What was she doing?

I hope she's made friends, Flora thought. *I hope she's as happy as I am.*

One morning there was a letter for Pogo at the breakfast table. When she read it, she let out a cry of joy. "It's from Neville! He's staying with some chums from his college – he says they're only about three miles away from here!" She looked shyly at Lady Badger. "Would you mind if my brother came to see me?"

Lady Badger said she would be delighted to meet him. "And ask him for tea, dear. Young men are always hungry. Will that be all right, Dorsey?"

"Hmm, I don't know," said Dorsey. "I don't generally approve of young men."

By now they all knew Dorsey well enough to know that this meant yes. Pogo hastily scribbled a postcard, inviting Neville to tea the day after next, and they cycled down to the village post office to send it off. Flora was glad he was coming. He was nice, and it was ages since she had talked to a man – at St Winifred's it was sometimes hard to remember that men existed at all.

They heard Neville before they saw him – his motorbike

roared along the quiet lanes and through the gates, before coughing to a halt outside the front porch.

"Nev!" Pogo cried. "How frabjous!"

Neville hopped off his motorbike – he had Pogo's quick, neat way of moving – slapped his sister's skinny back, and shook hands with her three best friends.

"Well, this is a piece of luck – I could hardly believe it when I found you were going to be so close. Crikey, what a view!" He smiled his friendly monkey-smile at Dulcie. "This place is beautiful. It's awfully decent of your grandmother to invite me."

"Come and meet everyone." Pogo grabbed his hand and tugged him into the house.

Lady Badger and Virginia were sitting in the grand but shabby drawing room. Paul and Silas instantly jumped up and threw themselves at Neville, and Lady Badger had to say, "Sit, you naughty boys! Sit!" several times, before the dogs went back to their place in front of the fire.

"Oh, Mr Lawrence, I'm terribly sorry – how very nice to meet you, dear."

"And this is Virginia Denning," Pogo said. "She's in the sixth. She's here to get over the measles, just like me and Dulcie."

"Hello." Neville shook Virginia's hand.

"It's not time for tea yet," said Lady Badger. "Why don't you girls take Mr Lawrence down to the beach?

And you should go too, Virginia. I don't want to send you back to school with those pale cheeks."

"We'll take the dogs, if you like," Neville said cheerfully. "It seems mean to leave them behind."

"Oh, you are nice!" Lady Badger said, beaming just like Dulcie. "Especially when they've just covered you with hair!"

They left the house in a gang, with Paul and Silas circling round them. Virginia was quiet at first, but couldn't help laughing at the excitement of the dogs – and the excitement of Pete, who kept trying to turn cartwheels and falling in a heap.

"I'm here with a couple of chaps from my college," Neville said. "We've borrowed a cottage for a fortnight, and the general idea is that we're studying, but we'll probably spend most of our time reading detective stories."

The beach was the bottom of a flight of rickety wooden steps, and Neville offered Virginia his hand as if she was an adult. Flora thought Virginia looked pretty, with the wind blowing her dark hair into her eyes. Neville seemed to think so too. He took his jacket off and spread it on a rock for her to sit on. At home in the future, Flora would've said that he fancied Virginia, but nobody talked about fancying in the 1930s.

It was weird to think that Virginia might fancy

Neville, and it made Flora a little shy with him. But this wore off when he began a lively game of throwing sticks into the waves for the dogs to fetch, and Flora and the other girls were soon soaking wet. He could skim pebbles so they bounced across the water, and they all tried to copy him, until it was time to troop back to the house for tea. He seemed to have injected them all with energy.

"Look at the state of you!" Dorsey groaned. "Don't you go trailing all that sand anywhere near my tea table!" She ordered the four girls off to the cloakroom to wash it off, which took some time owing to the ton of sand in Pete's hair. When they arrived at the table, Neville was in the middle of telling Lady Badger and Virginia about how he had been thrown into the fountain in his college because he was a communist.

"I'm a threat to the old order, you see. They won't accept that the world's changing and the old order's dead. Sooner or later, the workers will rise up to reclaim the means of production. The Russians have shown us the way."

He ate a mountain of crab sandwiches, three scones and two large slices of fruit cake, and told Dorsey she was a genius. "I ought to kidnap you and take you back to our wretched cottage – none of us can cook anything except baked beans."

Dorsey was so pleased that she pretended to be

furious and wrapped more slices of cake in greaseproof paper, for Neville to take back to his friends.

"Well, Pogo," Lady Badger said, after he had left, "what a charming young man. Do ask him again."

Over the next week, the last week of the girls' holiday, Neville visited every day. He brought his two friends over once — a very loud and jolly occasion — but mostly he came on his own, to mess about on the beach with the girls. Lady Badger grew fond of him, and said it was nice to have a man about the place again. He often talked about politics, and alarmed Dorsey with his predictions. One afternoon, he told her that when the revolution happened, the King would have to be executed, and Dorsey was deeply insulted. "This is a respectable country. Things like that don't happen here."

Lady Badger said she was interested in the revolution. "What will happen to me, Neville, dear?"

"Frightfully sorry, Lady B.," Neville said. "I'm afraid you'll be strung up from the nearest lamp post."

"Oh, but there aren't any lamp posts here," she said comfortably. "You'll have to shoot me."

"Don't worry," Flora said, with her mouth full of chocolate cake. "There won't be a revolution."

"You sound very certain," Virginia said. "How do you know?"

Pete gave her a warning pinch on the leg, and Flora felt her face turning hot. She had blurted it out without thinking. "I just – I don't think – it's not very likely, is it?"

Neville was interested. "It's possible, though – that's enough to go on for the moment. Obviously, I don't really want to shoot people. But there will jolly well have to be some way of making things fairer. We can't have any more children going without shoes, or people dying because they can't pay for doctors."

"People won't have to pay for doctors in the future," Flora couldn't resist saying. "It'll all be free, no matter how poor you are."

Neville whistled. "You're an optimist, Flora. I doubt any of us will live to see that."

Flora wanted to say "wait and see", but Pogo was giving her warning looks, so she shut up.

"I thought you were going to give away the whole shooting match!" Pogo said that night, when they were all undressing for bed. "In a way I wish we could tell Nev about you coming from the future – he's always talking about all the things that are going to happen when the workers rise up, whatever that actually means."

"They haven't risen up yet," Flora said. "A lot of the future isn't all that different to now – except that people are allowed to do more. You can stay up late and get divorced and dye your hair, and nobody cares."

"I think it sounds exciting," Pogo said. "I can't wait to live in a world where girls can be judges and prime ministers when they grow up. We're hardly allowed to be anything at the moment."

"Well, I think the future sounds rather frightening," Dulcie said. "And I wish we could tell Neville about it – I bet he'd know all the right questions to ask."

"Yes, but I might not know how to answer them," Flora pointed out.

Pete turned a somersault on her bed, and rolled off it with a loud thump. "OW! Neville wouldn't want to talk about the future, anyway. All he wants to do is stare at Virginia."

"Shut up, you beast!" Pogo threw her pillow at Pete.

"I think it's very romantic," Dulcie said. "They'll probably get married. I hope communists are allowed to have bridesmaids. I've always wanted to be one."

They were all giggling. It was true, Neville and Virginia always seemed to be apart from the group, sometimes holding hands when they thought nobody was looking.

"Gosh," Pogo said. "I can't quite imagine old Nev being in love!"

Pete suddenly let out a squawk of laughter. "I say – we can go ahead with that spell for Ethel now!"

"What are you talking about?"

"Don't you remember? We promised Ethel we'd cast

a spell to find her a rich husband. The one in the book says we need a hair each from the heads of true lovers! Well, we've got the lovers now, haven't we?"

"I thought we'd stopped doing magic," Dulcie said doubtfully.

Pogo finished buttoning her pyjamas, and pulled her small overnight bag from under the bed. She had brought the spellbook with her. They hadn't liked to leave it under the floorboards, where the fumigator men might find it. "Here it is. I suppose there's no harm in looking it up."

"I'd like to do something for Ethel," Flora said, remembering how kind she'd been on her dreadful first day. "As long as it's not dangerous."

Pogo opened the book at the chapter about Love. "An incantation to make a wealthy match for a Dowerless Maid," she read. "Yes, that's the one. 'Dowerless' means poor, and Ethel's poor. Her father's a farm labourer, and they all live in a tiny cottage over at the edge of Compton Wood." She studied the spell. "You're right, Pete – it does call for the hairs of true lovers. We also need a sprig of common samphire, a leaf of moneywort, some snail spittle—"

"Yuck!" said Flora. "How do you get a snail to spit, anyway?"

"It means the trail they leave, it's not like dribble. Hmm."

They were all quiet, looking at Pogo. She was wearing her thinking frown.

"Well?" Pete asked impatiently.

Pogo put the old book back in her bag. "It looks perfectly possible. And I've just realized that tomorrow would be an ideal time to do it. Virginia's going to the market with Dorsey and Lady B., and Nev's going to meet them there. We'll be free as air until tea."

They began the search for ingredients next morning, as soon as the car had taken Virginia, Lady Badger and Dorsey off to the nearest market town. Pete had come up with all kinds of outrageous plots to get the lovers' hairs, but Pogo said, "I'll snitch one of Nev's hairs at teatime, and we'll take one of Virginia's out of her comb. It's the snail spittle I'm worried about — and does anyone know what moneywort looks like?"

The samphire was a kind of spiky seaweed that grew among the flat rocks under the cliffs, and was easy to find. The snail-spit problem was solved when they stopped in a wood to eat their lunch, and Dulcie found a damp place criss-crossed with their silvery tracks. You couldn't pick these up, but Pogo wiped her handkerchief across them several times, and they all agreed that this would do.

In the afternoon the sun was almost as warm as summer, and they cycled to a place called Thurleston

Sands. Pogo bought them each a bottle of ginger beer, which Flora thought horrible – like a fizzy drink flavoured with black pepper. The wide, sandy beach was almost deserted, and they had such a great time paddling and racing the waves that they had to hurry to be back at Merrythorpe in time for tea.

Pete, who had set her heart on casting Ethel's spell, found the moneywort by simply asking Lady Badger's gardener. "Excuse me, Archer – what does moneywort look like?"

He showed them to a patch of ground in the shade of the garden wall, where flat, round leaves were spreading across the cracked stone ground.

Pogo snatched one of her brother's short brown hairs while they were pretending to fight before tea. She showed it to the others afterwards, stored in an old envelope. "Now all we need is a box of matches and an earthenware bowl – a pudding basin will do, Dulcie. You can sneak into the pantry while Dorsey's clearing the table."

For once, they were impatient to go up to bed. Flora had never performed a real spell before, and was almost giddy with nerves. The excitement made them all giggly. Pogo placed the earthenware pudding basin in the middle of the bedroom floor. Into it, she put the two hairs, the samphire and moneywort. The snail spit was more of a problem – it seemed to have disappeared. They shook Dulcie's handkerchief over the bowl and hoped it would work.

"Is that it?" Flora was disappointed. The ingredients at the bottom of the bowl looked like nothing but a couple of dirty leaves. "What happens now?"

Pogo consulted the old spellbook. "It says all persons present must chant the incantation, so you lot squash round where you can read it. We have to put in Ethel's name after 'Dowerless Maid' – her full name, just to be sure. And then we drop a live cinder into the bowl – we'll use a lighted match."

The other three girls pressed close to Pogo, and slowly chanted out the spell (quietly, because they didn't want anyone else, particularly Dorsey, hearing them).

> *"Spirit of Love, we entreat you,*
> *Come to aid*
> *The Dowerless Maid ETHEL MUNNS.*
> *With samphire we find thee,*
> *With lovers' hairs we bind thee;*
> *Snail spittle for silver,*
> *Moneywort for gold,*
> *Bring wealth without limit*
> *And happiness untold."*

Flora felt breathless and solemn. They watched in

silence as Pete struck the match and dropped it into the bowl.

"It's gone out," Dulcie whispered.

"No – look!" Flora could see a wisp of smoke, as thin as a thread. It rose out of the bowl in a straight column, then suddenly vanished. "Was that it? How do we know if it's worked?"

They all stood staring doubtfully at the heap of cinders at the bottom of the bowl, and then Dulcie suddenly farted – and the four of them erupted into screams of laughter. They laughed so hard that Lady Badger appeared in the doorway.

"My dear girls! Get into bed at once – before Dorsey hears you!"

Luckily, she did not see the bowl on the floor. Trying to swallow their giggles, the four girls climbed into their beds.

Pete moved her camp bed so that she was right beside Flora. "I'm so glad you came to the past," she whispered. "I hope it's ages till you have to do your task, so you can stay with us as long as possible. Isn't it ripping that we're such pals?"

"Yes," Flora whispered back, feeling very happy, "utterly corking!"

She didn't know that their friendship was about to be tested to the limit.

16

The Wrong Side of Pete

"Isn't it beastly to be back in prison again?" Pete sighed. At the end of their first full day back at St Winifred's, it was warm enough to sit out in the garden after tea. Pete had bagged one of the best places, on the lawn under the acacia tree.

"I don't mind," Pogo said. "There are so many nice things about the summer term — I can't wait for the cricket to start."

The smell of warm grass gave Flora a swift, sharp memory of drinking Diet Coke in Ella's garden. "I think I'm quite glad to be back," she said. "It feels nearer to my real home, somehow. This is where the magic has to happen."

"I don't think magic works at Merrythorpe,"

Dulcie said. "Otherwise Ethel wouldn't be such a disappointment."

"Oh, Dulcie," Pogo said kindly, "do stop going on about it! Did you really, truly expect to find Ethel married to King Cophetua?"

"Why not? It worked with Flora, didn't it? I didn't expect to come back and find that she's still just an ordinary parlour-maid."

"Perhaps she's already fallen in love, but it's a secret," Flora suggested.

"Oh no." Dulcie was firm. "A secret love would make her pale and thin."

Pete said, "You make it sound like an illness! When I fall in love, I want to be struck by a grand lightning bolt of passion – like Flora's granny was."

She was lying on her back with her long, spindly legs sprawled up the trunk of the tree. Her brown stockings were baggy and full of bad darns, and the others giggled – it was hard to picture her being struck by a bolt of passion.

Pete was haughty. "That's what she said, isn't it?"

"Oh, Granny's always going on about love and passion and stuff," Flora said. "When she met the artist guy, she ran away from her husband without even taking her toothbrush. She didn't take any money, either. The artist offered to buy her a diamond ring, and she said she'd rather have a few pairs of knickers."

"Gosh, she sounds divine!" The long legs swung down, and Pete sat up. She never got tired of hearing about Flora's granny's love life. "My grandmother looks like Queen Victoria – nobody on earth would want to paint her in the nude. You're so lucky!"

She'd said things like this before, and it was starting to make Flora feel uncomfortable. If her granny had belonged to someone else, wouldn't she want to know more about her? When she told other people about her adventures – the famous artist, the famous nude paintings of her in national art galleries – they were often really impressed. The boring holiday in Italy, and then the huge changes happening at home, had taken up too much of Flora's attention.

Let's face it, she thought, *I was too busy sulking to get to know Granny properly. Ella was the one who liked listening to her stories.* If she ever got home, she might give the old bat another try.

There were a lot of very nice things about the summer term. The evenings were longer and lighter, and the weather was warmer. The gardens were full of flowers and birds.

The teachers concentrated on the girls taking School Certificate (the old-fashioned version of GCSEs) and were far less strict with the lower forms. On warm afternoons, Mademoiselle Dornay taught her French class under the big acacia tree on the lawn, and Flora found it hard to think about verbs and tenses when there was a nest of thrushes on the branch above her, and caterpillars kept dropping on her book.

Miss Palmer, the English teacher, did less grammar in her lessons, and more poetry, which Flora liked. She had discovered that she was rather good at reciting poems. One morning, they did Lewis Carroll's "The Walrus and the Carpenter", which Flora knew well because Dad had read it to her when she was little. All the girls read different bits of the poem. The carpenter made Flora think of the gloomy old man who had built their kitchen in Wimbledon, and when she read: "'I doubt it,' said the Carpenter, and shed a bitter tear,'" in his deep, dragging voice, the class fell about laughing.

This was the beginning of all the trouble. Flora's performance gave Miss Palmer a brilliant idea.

"As you may know, I've been put in charge of the first form's contribution to our annual Speech Day display," she told them at their next English class. "This display will be seen by all the school governors and visiting parents on Speech Day – and I've decided to do 'The Walrus and the Carpenter'. Flora, I hope you'll give a repeat of that splendid performance. The other girls taking part will be Dorothy and Consuela. We'll be having our first rehearsal next week – I expect you three to know every word by heart."

Dulcie and Pogo grinned at Flora. Dulcie mouthed, "Well done!"

Pete stiffened with anger and bit her lower lip. Flora tried to catch her eye, but Pete refused to look in her direction. At the end of the class she scraped back her chair and flounced out ahead of everyone else. Flora and the others found her glowering in the corner of the common room.

"We're honoured," she sneered. "The star actress has deigned to join us! The great Flora Fox!"

"Pete," Dulcie said solemnly, "don't be mean to Flora just because you're jealous."

"Jealous? Of course I'm not jealous — she's welcome to wear a carpenter's hat and apron and make a fool of herself in front of the whole school! But I'm very angry with Miss Palmer, and I might have to tell my people to complain about her — choosing that babyish poem! And she said she was considering ME!"

Pogo sighed and rolled her eyes. "Oh, Pete — she didn't say that! You ASKED her to consider you, and she told you she might. But you didn't really think she'd allow you to do 'The Charge of the Light Brigade', did you?"

"It's my father's favourite poem," Pete said fiercely. "And she said my recitation was a great success!"

"Only because we all laughed so much," Dulcie said. "And it's not a poem you're supposed to laugh at — not

191

when it's about a lot of soldiers dying."

Flora was grateful that Pogo and Dulcie were sticking up for her. Pete's sudden anger was horrible.

"She should've given ME something to do in the display!" hissed Pete. "My mother and father are coming all the way from London for Speech Day – and Flora's people aren't even here!" She turned angrily to Flora. "You should've refused!"

"Don't be a chump," Pogo said. "Why should she? I've said it before, Pete – you're an utter monster when your royal nose is out of joint."

The table beside the window was empty. Pogo went to bag it, and calmly took out her prep. Whatever she was feeling inside, she was not a person to lose her cool. Flora wished she could be cool. When Dulcie had joined Pogo at the table, she lingered beside Pete.

"Look . . ." What on earth could she say? "Sorry I got chosen."

"Oh, don't APOLOGIZE!" huffed Pete. "Hadn't you better go and sit with the friends you STOLE from me?"

"Pete—"

"Ah, Flora." Consuela Carver was beside them. She gave Flora a superior smile. "How delightful that we'll be reciting together at Speech Day! Poor Pete – but you can see why she couldn't choose you."

Pete stood up and scowled into the Carver's face.

"What are you talking about?"

"Well, you lollop about, and you look such a hoyden – hardly an ornament to the school!"

Pete's face and neck turned deep red. "At least my people care about me," she said. "At least they love me enough to come to Speech Day – at least they're not DIVORCED!"

"Pete!" Flora was horrified – this was incredibly mean. Who had told Pete? She didn't want the Carver to think she had broken her promise.

Consuela choked something that sounded like, "Beast!"

She swung her satchel and hit Pete hard on the head – it made a sickening thud. Pete was knocked to the floor.

Every other girl in the room was suddenly silent, staring in amazement. After a dazed moment of rubbing her head, Pete scrambled to her feet and smacked Consuela's face.

"Don't!" Flora cried.

Pete and the Carver were fighting for real now – scratching and kicking and hair pulling. Flora and a couple of other girls nearby tried to pull them apart, but the flying fists drove them back. More girls stepped in, grabbing any bit of the fighters they could get hold of, and this made them fight harder. The common room was a pandemonium of shouts and shrieks.

The door opened with a crash. The small, shrivelled figure of Miss Harbottle stood in the doorway. The girls were all quiet now. Consuela and Pete allowed the other girls to pull them apart. The sleeve of Pete's blouse was torn. Consuela's nose was bleeding.

In deathly silence, Harbottle stomped into the middle of the room. She was furious.

"I have NEVER seen anything so DISGRACEFUL! Fighting like a pair of GUTTERSNIPES! It's enough to make Miss Beak turn in her grave!" She scowled at the two girls. "Someone give the Carver gel a handkerchief."

Flora, standing nearest, fished her hanky from her knicker leg and gave it to Consuela.

"YOU, Miss Carver!" snapped Harbottle. "Why do I find YOU at the centre of every drama, I wonder? Someone tell me what happened." The beady little eyes travelled round the roomful of quailing girls. "Cecilia Lawrence!"

Pogo was still at the table beside the window. "Yes, Miss Harbottle."

"Who provoked this revolting exhibition?"

"I – I didn't really see all of it."

"Tell me what you DID see!"

"I saw Consuela hit Pete – Daphne."

Harbottle turned fiercely back to Consuela. "Is this true?"

Consuela dabbed at her bleeding nose with Flora's

handkerchief. "Yes."

"Would you care to tell me WHY?"

She was pale. "No, Miss Harbottle."

"I see. You attacked Daphne for no reason at all."

"Yes," said Consuela. "No."

Harbottle's wrinkles folded into a scowl. "This is RIDICULOUS. Either you had a reason, or you did not."

"She did." Flora couldn't help saying – she was still shocked by Pete's nastiness. "Pete said something."

There were gasps, and someone let out a nervous giggle.

"Well, well, well," croaked Harbottle, "the barrack-room lawyer speaks again! Can you tell me what was said?"

Pete was glaring at Flora – and so was Consuela. Neither of them wanted her to say it.

Flora said, "No, I can't. But it was a really good reason to hit someone."

"Hmm," said Harbottle. "I am inclined to take your word for it. Daphne and Consuela, you are both at fault, and you will both report to me after tea." She walked out of the hushed room, slamming the door behind her.

A little cautious talking broke out. Everyone moved away from Flora, Pete and Consuela.

Pete gave Flora a murderous look, and flounced away to the table in the window.

Consuela also gave her a murderous look. "I suppose YOU told her!"

I can't win, Flora thought.

She was shaken. In a few short minutes, the whole atmosphere of the day had turned poisonous. Pete suddenly hated her, and being on the wrong side of Pete was horrible.

"You're an ungrateful beast, Flora Fox! I've done everything for you! How DARE you stick up for the Carver? A fine friend you are!" Pete exploded as soon as they got to the bedroom. "Thanks to you I got a ton of extra prep from Harbottle – and a double pony! My only consolation is that you'll look IDIOTIC at Speech Day and make a complete bish of it!"

Pogo said, "Stop it. She was only telling the truth."

"Look, I don't like Consuela any more than you do," Flora said, "but you shouldn't have been such a cow to her – no wonder she decked you! And if she got blamed for starting the fight, it just wouldn't be fair!"

"Talk to the hand, kitchenmaid!" snapped Pete, "because the face is NEVER SPEAKING TO YOU EVER AGAIN!" She pulled the curtains of her cubicle shut, so violently that several of the rings broke.

"Oh dear," said Dulcie. "It doesn't look as if she's going to come round this time."

Pogo was very thoughtful. She looked sharply from

the curtained bed to Flora, as if making up her mind. "You're right. It wouldn't have been fair not to speak up for the Carver. I don't know about you two, but I don't much like Miss Peterson at the moment. In my humble opinion, Miss Peterson is a conceited ass!"

They all went to bed in very low spirits. Flora lay awake in the shadows for ages. She had lost another best friend. First Ella, now Pete.

But last time it was my fault, she thought, *and this time it's not. How can I make it right again?*

She drifted into sorrowful sleep, and had a very strange dream.

A voice was calling her name. It rang out through the silent, sleeping school. *"Flora! Flora!"*

She dreamed that she got out of bed and went down the great staircase to the hall.

"Flora!" The voice was cross and crabby, and vaguely familiar.

Someone was waiting for her beside the fireplace, under the portrait of Dame Mildred Beak. This person was wearing school uniform, but she had her back turned, and Flora couldn't see who it was. She walked towards her uncertainly.

The figure suddenly whipped round, and Flora gasped, "Granny!"

The gymslip looked grotesque on Granny's stooped old body. She glared haughtily at Flora, just as she had done last summer in Italy.

From above the fireplace came a rumbling sound, like low thunder. The portrait of Dame Mildred slowly turned its head and gazed down at them.

In a distant, echoing voice, Dame Mildred said, "If you two cannot be friends, you will never know."

"Know what?" Flora asked.

But the bell rang and woke her, before the old sorceress could explain.

17

Hare and Hounds

Nobody could keep up a sulk like Pete. Two whole weeks after the fight with Consuela, she was still refusing to speak to Flora. She was also refusing to speak to Pogo and Dulcie, which made the bedroom very uncomfortable. Normally, when Pete was in one of her moods, Pogo said, "Ignore her. She'll come round." This time, however, she wasn't so forgiving. She had told Pete she was a "conceited ass", and she was sticking to it.

"It's time she learned the difference between right and wrong," she told Flora sharply. "She refuses to see why what she said to Consuela went beyond the limit. She won't admit that it was – well – cruel. She's too lazy to look at another person's point of view." She added, "I wrote to Neville for his opinion – not naming names, but I bet he knew whom I meant – and that's what he said. He said she's like people who prefer to think the poor are careless, so they don't have to think about why poverty exists."

They were talking while they changed for games. This afternoon, the lower school was to play something called hare and hounds, which involved cross-country running. The girls gathered on the patch of gravel at the front of the school. Miss Gatling, the games teacher (a strapping woman, with bad cellulite on her upper arms), organized them into two groups and handed out red and blue sashes.

"Pay attention, girls. The reds are hares, and the rest of you are hounds. The hares will have a ten-minute start. They will leave a paper trail, and the hounds must try to catch them before they reach the finishing point, which is the village post office."

Pete and Pogo, both fast runners, were hares. Flora and Dulcie were among the crowd of hounds.

"I don't much like this game," Dulcie confessed. "There's so much mud, and you get so tired. And I wish it wasn't raining."

"It's not raining hard," Flora said. She was rather looking forward to roaming through the countryside without a teacher breathing down her neck. She missed the freedom they'd had at Merrythorpe. And she also missed her light, soft trainers – they would have made a cross-country run so much easier.

"One more thing!" called Miss Gatling. "You may go anywhere inside the designated area – but Compton Wood is out of bounds. There's been a landslip at the old quarry, and the farmer says it isn't safe. You'll have to skirt round it. And latecomers lose team points – so no slacking!"

The hares, with their big bags of paper slung over their shoulders, lined up on the path. Miss Gatling blew her whistle, and they dashed away along the drive. Ten minutes later, the whistle blew again, and the crowd of hounds ran after them.

Flora ran as fast as she could, but she and Dulcie soon fell behind the faster girls. When the trail left the road and veered off through coppices and fields, they had a hard time keeping up. Dulcie eventually collapsed on a stone wall. "I can't walk another step, let alone run. And we haven't seen a single scrap of paper – where are all the others?"

Flora knew the countryside immediately around St Winifred's from all the nature rambles and botany field trips they had done this term. "They'll have to go over Crow Hill, since we can't take the short cut through the wood. Come on, Dulcie – we'll get left behind!"

Dulcie sighed. "I've got a beastly blister on my heel. You go on, and I'll catch you up when I've had a rest."

Sweet-natured as she was, Dulcie could be stubborn. She had made up her mind, and she was not going to budge.

"OK," Flora said. "We last saw the others going up that bank – see you later."

She set off at a brisk walking pace. On the other side of the grassy bank ahead, there was the big, green sweep of Crow Hill. At the top of the hill was the forbidden Compton Wood, which stood between the runners and their meeting point at the post office. What path had the hares taken? The light was turning dull. Flora paused to stare at the hillside, with its thin trail of white paper.

In the distance, two girls were running – one determined hound in a blue sash, chasing one hare. Flora thought she recognized Pete. How had she managed to get so far behind the other hares?

She'll catch it from Miss Gatling, Flora thought.

Crikey – Pete had run straight into the wood. Now she really would catch it.

A few seconds later, the hound ran right in after her. Flora couldn't see who it was, and she was too far off to shout at. She set off up the hill as fast as she could. Of course it was tempting to take the short cut, like Pete and the other girl, but she wasn't sure she knew the way through the wood, and it was big enough to get lost in. At the top of the hill, she saw one piece of white paper stuck to a bush, showing the path she had to take. The afternoon was fading, and she was starting to think about tea.

She was just guessing that Pete would have been caught by the hound by now, and would be nearly at the finishing point – when Pete herself suddenly walked out of a clump of trees, right in front of her.

The two girls stared at each other.

"Krupp!" said Pete crossly. "I suppose this means I've been captured – after all my hard work!"

"But I thought you'd been captured ages ago," Flora said. "Where's the other girl?"

"And it would have to be you. You're just determined to spoil every single thing I do."

"I saw someone running into the trees behind you," Flora said.

Pete shrugged impatiently. "Well, she didn't get me, and you did. Come on. Let's get to the wretched post office." She started off across the grass.

"Wait!" Flora was uneasy, though she didn't know exactly why. It was as if someone had told her the answer to something important, without telling her the question. "I did see someone following you – shouldn't we wait for her?"

"What for?"

"I don't know." The strange, uneasy feeling was growing. "To make sure she's OK."

"Why wouldn't she be? Come on!"

"You go on," Flora said. "I'll wait here for a minute. If she doesn't come out, I'll start looking for her."

Pete rolled her eyes. "All right, I did see someone. It was Consuela – your new bosom friend. But she didn't see me. I wasn't going to get myself caught by the likes of her!"

"Can't you forget your silly feud for a second?" Flora looked at Pete's angry face, and did not like her one bit. How could she ever have liked her? She could swear she was hiding something. "Consuela might be lost. She might be hurt."

"Well, we can just tell Miss Gatling. If she's sprained her ankle it won't hurt her to wait for a few minutes."

"Pete! I don't believe you sometimes!" Flora was afraid. All her instincts told her something was wrong. Pete looked incredibly shifty. "What are you talking about? What sprained ankle?"

"ALL RIGHT!" Pete shouted. "I saw her slip into the quarry – satisfied?"

"No! How did she get out?"

"I don't know."

"What do you mean? You didn't just leave her there!"

Pete's scowl deepened. "I didn't want to get captured!"

"I'm going to look for her!" Flora turned and

followed the overgrown path into the wood. She called Consuela's name – loudly enough to make the birds fly out of the branches above her – but there was no reply. "Consuela!"

Pete ran to catch up with her. "All right, I'll come with you, since you can't stop nagging. But she's probably just sulking."

"She fell into the quarry – and you left her," Flora said furiously. "All because you didn't want to lose a point in a stupid game! Where've you been, anyway? How come you got left behind by the other hares?"

"If you must know, Miss Goody Two-Shoes, I got out of breath, so I hid up a tree until all the hounds had gone past."

"Shh a minute—" Flora grabbed Pete's hand. "I think I heard something!"

"What?"

"Shhh!"

They both stood still, letting the silence settle around them, and Flora heard the sound again – a faint cry, like an animal at the end of its strength.

This time, Pete had to come off it and admit that something was really wrong. She ran along the twisting path through the trees, towards the old quarry, with Flora close behind her. The quarry was a huge clearing in the middle of the wood. The stone ground had been dug out into a crater at least thirty feet deep.

Flora looked over the edge. At the bottom of the pit, a still figure lay beside a heap of loose rocks. "Consuela!"

Consuela's leg was twisted at an odd, sickening angle. Flora looked round frantically for a way to get down to her without slipping – as the farmer had warned, there were loose stones scattered everywhere. If she put her foot in the wrong place, she could easily slip right down to the depths.

Pete had turned very pale, and was no longer being a pain. Even she could tell this was an emergency. "One of us should go down to her, and one of us should run for help."

"But help from where?" wailed Flora. "The school's miles away!"

"I know," Pete said. "Ethel's house – it's easily the nearest—" She turned and pelted away down the path.

Flora was alone now. She looked doubtfully at the steep sides of the quarry. If she fell to her death in the past – but she couldn't afford to start thinking like this, or she would panic.

"Help!" Consuela cried feebly.

"I'm coming!" Flora called. "Stay there!"

What an idiotic thing to say, when Consuela had no choice. Flora walked around the edge of the crater, until she found a place where the sides were less steep, and there was a sort of path down to the bottom. Some of the stones were loose, and there was a hairy moment when she sent a large rock crashing down, but she told herself to imagine she was climbing on the cliffs at Merrythorpe and managed not to stumble.

Consuela lay in a huddle. Her face was an awful greyish white, striped with tears. Flora gingerly took her cold hand, and she turned her head.

"Flora?" she murmured.

"Yes, it's me – someone'll be here to rescue you in a minute." She hoped this was true. Could the abominable Pete really be trusted with something so important?

"I think I've broken my leg – it really hurts! I'm not going to die, am I?"

"No, of course not." Flora squeezed Consuela's hand. "My mum broke her leg last year when we went skiing, and she's fine now." She had forgotten what century she was in – where would the other Flora's mother have gone skiing in British India?

"Truly?" Consuela was too dazed with pain to notice. "Mummy won't like it if I have a limp."

Her mother sounded like a cow. Flora thought of Mum in the twenty-first century, and had to swallow hard so she wouldn't start crying. "Truly," she said. "You won't have even a bit of a limp."

Where was Pete? How were they going to get Consuela out of the quarry? Did they have helicopter ambulances in 1935 – did they even have helicopters?

The light was fading, and Consuela had gone very quiet. Flora shifted to a more comfortable position. There was nothing she could do but wait.

There were lights at the top of the quarry, and voices.

"Flora! Are you all right?"

"Hold on, Miss – we're coming!"

A few loose stones crashed to the ground. Someone with a lantern was stumbling down the steep path, towards Flora and Consuela. It was Ethel, unfamiliar in a flowered dress and cardigan. And after her came her dad, Mr Munns, and her brother Ron, carrying ropes and sheets and an old door they were using as a stretcher. Flora was so glad to see them that she forgot about 1930s girls not hugging and threw her arms round Ethel.

As Pete said later, Ethel was a "trump". She soothed poor Consuela, stroking her forehead while her father and brother strapped her to the makeshift stretcher. She helped them carry it up the path as slowly and smoothly as possible.

The cottage where Ethel's family lived was tiny, and packed with people. Ethel's mum, Mrs Munns, was a tall, solid woman, in a huge apron, with a loud voice that never stopped rapping out instructions.

"Bring her in the parlour – that's it, I've pulled out the couch – don't you fret, my duck, I've sent Lizzie to

208

tell the school, and little Ernie's run for Dr Whitty – Eth, get these girls a cup of hot tea – careful, Ron! Don't go jolting and jouncing the poor little love! What's her name? Consuela – well, that's pretty – can you hear me, Consuela? I know it hurts, but what a brave girl you are! I've always said that quarry was a danger – Dad, put on a pan of hot water, the doctor always seems to want it—"

Flora found herself squashed into a hot corner beside the fireplace next to Pete, drinking a cup of sweet tea.

"And you two," Mrs Munns said, "aren't you lovely girls, to go looking for your friend? I don't hardly like to think what would've happened if you hadn't!"

"I'm ever so glad this is my day off," Ethel said. She smiled into Consuela's face. "Now I can hold your hand right through, and not leave you for a single minute."

She was a very kind girl, and it made her pretty face absolutely beautiful, Flora thought.

Pete was silent and pale, more shaken than Flora had ever seen her. It was slightly surprising that she was so freaked out.

Flora whispered, "Pete, are you OK?"

Pete only nodded, and wouldn't look Flora in the eye.

Flora did not understand – was she in shock? "What's up?" she hissed to Pete. "Are you going to faint, or something?"

"No."

Mrs Munns was trying to clear the tiny room. She had only just shooed Ethel's brothers and sisters upstairs, however, when there was another commotion. A car was heard in the lane outside. A skinny little girl of about nine burst in, gabbling something about a man and a big car – Flora guessed this must be Lizzie, who had run to St Winifred's.

Miss Bradley appeared in the doorway. "Consuela – you poor child! Mrs Munns, this is tremendously good of you—"

"Is she here?" a man's voice asked behind her. "Is she going to be all right?"

Miss Bradley stood aside and a tall man came in. He was dressed in a black suit that looked glossy and expensive, and he filled the small room with a scent of lemon soap. He knelt down beside Consuela. "My darling!"

She opened her eyes. "Daddy?"

"Don't worry about anything, darling. I'm here now."

Consuela stared at him, as if she didn't believe her eyes. "But – you're in Kenya!"

"I didn't tell you I was coming," he said, "because I didn't know if your mother would let me see you. But I have the best possible news – she signed a piece of paper this morning, which means you're coming to live with me!"

Wow, thought Flora, *this is as good as magic, and we didn't even cast a spell*.

She caught Consuela's dazed eye, and gave her a huge smile.

"Well, you two pickles!" Miss Bradley said cheerfully. "You've had the entire school in an uproar, and given poor Miss Gatling the fright of her life! We were just setting out to search for the three of you when Lizzie came dashing in – and just as the head was telephoning for an ambulance, Mr Carver suddenly turned up – talk about a night to remember!"

"It was my fault," Pete said loudly. "Consuela only went into the wood because she was following me."

"Never mind about that now, dear. The ambulance is coming to take Consuela to the nursing home, and you two must get back to school."

Consuela murmured, "Couldn't I stay here with Ethel?" She was still gripping Ethel's hand.

Mrs Munns laughed. "Bless you, duck, you'd be welcome if I had the space!"

Mr Carver looked at Ethel, and said, "I can't thank you enough."

"And don't forget to thank these two young ladies," said Mrs Munns. "They went searching for Consuela the minute they missed her – didn't even wait to tell the teacher."

Mr Carver stood up and solemnly shook hands with

Flora and Pete. "Thanks awfully. I'm jolly glad Consuela has such first-rate pals."

Pete hung her head, as if he had told her off instead of thanking her – Flora couldn't understand it. She didn't even cheer up when they were driven back to St Winifred's in Mr Carver's gorgeous car. It was long and low and sleek, and the inside smelled like a posh suitcase. Miss Bradley rode in front beside the driver, because she wanted to look at the dashboard. The back seat was sealed off with a panel of glass.

Flora leaned back luxuriously. "I could get used to this! Pete? What's the matter with you? Are you ill?"

Pete buried her face in her hands and burst into tears.

"Pete?" Flora tried to put her arm around her, but she shrugged away.

"Don't – you don't know what I've done!"

"What're you talking about?"

Pete whispered, "I – I pushed her!"

18

A Credit to the School

The shock was like a punch in the stomach. It was a moment or two before Flora could speak. "You mean – by accident?"

"No!" Pete cried passionately. "I pushed her on purpose!" She was sobbing. Flora tried to put her arm round her, but she shrugged it away. "Don't be nice to me. I don't deserve it. I could've killed her!"

"But Pete – crikey – what got into you?"

"I don't know – if I'd stopped to think about it – look, Flora, I know how beastly I am. I can't talk about it any more – I'll tell you later, but I can't do it now." She turned her face away.

"OK." Flora was worried to the point of being seriously freaked out. It wasn't just that Pete had done something dreadful. She had never seen the swaggering, super-confident Pete like this – weeping and shaking, shut up inside herself.

It was dark when they arrived back at St Winifred's. In the hall, Pete suddenly grabbed Miss Bradley's sleeve.

"I have to see the headmistress," she said loudly.

"It's far too late now, dear."

"Please, Miss Bradley – I have to see her now! It's a matter of life and death! Please!"

Miss Bradley was startled by her fierceness. "Surely it can wait until morning?"

"It has to be now – I have something very important to tell her."

"Very well, if you insist. Flora, you go upstairs."

Flora tried to catch Pete's eye, but Pete refused to look at her. Her face was pale and scared, and stiff with determination.

Miss Bradley knocked on the door of Miss Powers-Prout's study. A distant voice called, "Enter!" and the door swallowed them up.

Was she going to confess everything to the head – even the fact that she had pushed Consuela? What would happen to her? Flora went up to the bedroom, where she found Dulcie and Pogo agog to hear the story.

"Where have you been? Is it true you saved the Carver's life?" Dulcie bounced on her bed eagerly. "The whole school's talking about it!"

Flora was very tired, and suddenly aware that she ached all over. She had tripped a couple of times while climbing out of the quarry, and hadn't noticed the bruises until now. She sat down on her bed and peeled off her very muddy games shirt. "Pete's with the head."

Pogo whistled. "Golly – what's all that about? Is she in hot water again?"

"I'm not sure. Let's wait till she comes up." Flora didn't want to tell the others what Pete had told her. She changed into the other Flora's pyjamas and went to wash her face and brush her teeth in the deserted cloakroom. Pete was not in the bedroom when she came back, and it was getting near lights out.

Dulcie said, "What's Pete done now? Can she be expelled in the middle of the night?"

"Steady on," said Pogo. "We don't know that anyone's being expelled."

The door opened slowly, and they all fell silent as Pete walked in. Her face was swollen with tears. She looked somehow smaller all over. When she spoke, her voice was flat and defeated.

"I suppose Flora's told you."

"I haven't said a thing," Flora said quickly.

"Thanks."

"Told us what?" demanded Pogo.

"You might not want to be friends with me any

more," Pete said. "And – and I wouldn't blame you."

Her head bowed, she told them the whole story about Consuela following her into Compton Wood.

"I didn't want her to catch me, so I hid from her. She was calling to me – 'I know you're here' – and she went right to the edge of the quarry. I could've just run away from her, and I do wish I had now – but I was tired and I didn't want to run any more. All I could think was how much I didn't like Consuela, and how she'd crow when she caught me – so I ran up behind her and gave her a shove. And she fell into the quarry."

Dulcie's blue eyes were wide with horror. "Oh, Pete! You didn't!"

"Crikey!" Pogo said. "That's pretty good, even for you."

"If it hadn't been for Flora," Pete said, "I would have left Consuela lying there. I meant to mention it to Miss Gatling if she didn't turn up. I didn't know she was so badly hurt – not that it's an excuse. She might have died because of what I did. I saw it all in a flash when we found her and she looked all peculiar and crooked. All the time I was running to Ethel's, I was seeing myself for the very first time, and it was perfectly horrible. I'm such a selfish beast that I nearly killed someone. That's why I had to see Old Peepy. I had to own up to the whole thing straight away."

216

"I'd never dare!" squeaked Dulcie. "What did she say? Was it hideous?"

The ten-minute bell sounded. Pete went to her bed and began to take off her clothes. "She was pretty decent, actually – but only after I'd told her every single thing. I told her it was all my fault, and I asked her not to be angry with anyone else. And I told her what a trump you were, Flora. Thanks awfully." With her blouse half on and half off, she came across the room, holding out her hand. "I don't deserve a chum like you."

Solemnly, Pete and Flora shook hands.

Pete then turned to Pogo and Dulcie. "I'm really sorry – about everything, really." She shook hands with the other two girls.

"Gosh, Pete!" Pogo said. "I've never seen you in sackcloth, but it suits you. What I mean is, I've never heard you admit to being wrong before. I may faint."

"We're still your chums," Dulcie assured her. "You didn't mean to do anything bad, and you've owned up like a brick."

"You lot are the bricks," Pete said gruffly. "I've been nothing but a bother to you – I've caused no end of trouble by summoning Flora. Is it pax?"

"Of course it's pax!" Impulsively, Flora flung her arms around Pete's lanky, dejected figure. "This is what we'd do in my century!"

After a startled second, Pete hugged her back. The two friends clung to each other, and Flora was suddenly incredibly happy, as if an invisible load had been lifted off her back.

"How disgustingly sentimental," said Pogo.

Life was wonderful. School was wonderful. Her friends were wonderful. "Shut up, Pogo!" yelled Flora. "Now we have to do a GROUP HUG — that means we all hug each other at the same time!"

"You future-girls are crazy — OW!" Flora and Pete both dragged Pogo and Dulcie into a real twenty-first century group hug — like the group hug her table at APS had done when they won the Christmas quiz.

Pete stumbled, and all four of them toppled to the floor in a mad tangle of limbs, screaming with laughter.

They laughed so much that Virginia came into the bedroom, holding her glasses in one hand and a letter in the other. "Nothing in the world is that funny," she said, "so pipe down, before you stir the Harbottle from her lair."

Dulcie said, "Sorry, Virginia."

When she had gone, and they had managed to stop giggling, Pete hurried into her pyjamas. "I didn't finish telling you about Old Peepy. She said she'd had a call from Consuela's father, to say thank you. Consuela doesn't remember anything except shouting for help and then waking up and seeing Flora. Old Peepy said I should leave it there, and not confess to anyone else. She – she said I'd been given a chance to atone for my wicked act, and she trusted me to punish myself." Her lip quivered, and her red eyes filled with tears. "You're all being jolly decent about this. I'll do my best not to be a pig any more."

Pogo said, "I think the piggish Pete has taken flight, and we won't be seeing any more of her. We're the Four Musketeers again – all for one and one for all – but no more group hugs!"

"You wouldn't like my century," Flora said, laughing. "There's a lot of hugging."

The bell rang. The girls climbed into their beds and switched off their lamps.

"Pssst!" hissed Pogo. "Did you see? Virginia was reading a letter from Neville – I'd know his writing anywhere."

They all giggled over this, before settling into silence.

Flora lay awake on her back, with one arm around the other Flora's bear, staring up at the ceiling. She was very tired, floating on a sea of calm. The whole world was calm. Something important had happened today. She remembered Pete saying, "I'm such a selfish beast that I nearly killed someone . . . if it hadn't been for Flora . . ."

And then it hit her. This was the "task" she had been summoned here to do. What else could explain this strange feeling of rightness, as if a machine part

219

had clicked into place? If she had not followed Pete and Consuela, if she had not insisted on going to look for Consuela, it might have been ages before anyone found her. For all anyone knew, she might have died — it was possible that the summoning spell had prevented the destruction of more than one life.

Did this mean she was about to go home to her own time? Even as she gasped aloud with longing and excitement, Flora seemed to know that it wouldn't be yet. The task wasn't quite done. She had a strong sense that there was something else to do first.

"Ah, Daphne — the very girl I wanted to see," Miss Palmer said. She stopped Pete and Flora in the hall after breakfast. "Speech Day is next week, and I don't think poor Consuela will be able to perform, so I'd like you to take her place."

"Gosh — I mean, thanks, Miss Palmer!" Colour rushed into Pete's cheeks. "If you think I'll be good enough."

Miss Palmer smiled. "I haven't forgotten your very amusing recital of 'The Charge of the Light Brigade'. Dorothy will take Consuela's part, and I need you to be the Walrus — you won't mind wearing whiskers, will you?"

"Rather not," said the new, non-troublemaking Pete. "And thanks awfully!"

"Splendid. Come along to my study after tea."

"Pete, that's so cool!" Flora blurted out, as soon as Miss Palmer had gone. "We'll be on stage together!"

"I can't believe it!" She grabbed Flora's hand. "I won't be as good as you – but won't we have fun?"

It was amazing to hear Pete saying something this modest, but yesterday's lesson had struck deep, and went on working over the following days. Pete was as light-hearted (and light-headed) as ever, but she was making a real effort to think about other people.

"She Who Must Be Obeyed is a lot nicer to live with nowadays," Pogo remarked. "She hasn't given me any orders for ages."

Flora was impressed by the amount of work Pete put into "The Walrus and the Carpenter". The old Pete hated practising anything. Frankly, the old Pete had always felt she was too naturally gifted to need practice. The new Pete, however, wanted to spend every spare minute practising. She dragged Flora and Dorothy into empty classrooms at all times of day, to go through the poem over and over again until the words were printed in Flora's dreams.

Speech Day at St Winifred's turned out to be a very big deal. There was an atmosphere of excitement, and everyone was on edge.

"Of course, none of you first-formers have seen a Speech Day at St Winifred's," Miss Bradley said, on the morning of the great day. "Well, it's quite an occasion. The teachers and the head sit on the platform, and we are all simply magnificent in our best academic regalia. Even Miss Harbottle wears a slightly newer gown. Then we all have to sit through the displays and the speeches, before being rewarded with an excellent tea."

The girls were to wear their "best" dresses of white silk. They found them hanging, freshly ironed, from the curtain rails of their beds, when they came upstairs to get changed.

"Yuck," said Flora, frowning at herself in the bedroom mirror, "I look like an overgrown four-year-old! Don't tell me they make the sixth-formers wear these?"

It was time for the girls not in the display to take their places in the assembly hall.

"Jolly good luck, you two," Pogo said. "We'll be cheering you from the audience." She and Dulcie left the room.

"Oh, why did I agree to do this?" groaned Pete. "I'm SO nervous! Suppose I forget my lines?"

Flora's stomach was fluttering with nerves, but she did her best to sound confident. "Don't be silly, we must've been through them a million times." She put on her carpenter's hat and apron. Miss Palmer had wanted them to look like the Tenniel illustrations in the book, and she had made Pete a huge pair of cardboard tusks and a brown wool moustache.

222

The two girls went downstairs, to wait with Dorothy behind a screen at the side of the platform – they weren't on until after the lower-school choir. The assembly hall was filling up now. Flora listened to the hum of talking, and the three girls took turns to peep out at the audience through a crack in the screen.

The girls sat on one side of the hall, in a solid block of white, and the parents sat on the other – Pete had to swallow a squeak of excitement when she saw her own mother and father.

Dorothy spotted her mother and her aunt, and groaned softly. "Aunt Nora's wearing the silliest hat – I may die of humiliation."

The school orchestra began to play (not very well) a stately march. Silence fell in the assembly hall, and the procession of teachers entered. As Miss Bradley had said, they looked splendid – they were all wearing new black gowns and square black hats. Miss Palmer and Mademoiselle Dornay wore lipstick, and Flora managed to notice, through her nerves, that they had all made efforts with their hair (yes, even Harbottle, who no longer looked as if she had a white bird's nest on her head).

The headmistress marched in last, tall and proud. Her chair, in the middle of the platform, was a kind of throne.

Her voice was gracious. "My Lord Bishop, governors

and parents, ladies and gentlemen," she began, with a nod to the bishop in the front row. "It is my great pleasure to welcome you all to St Winifred's on our annual Speech Day. This past year has been one of hard work and play, and we have had particular success . . ."

Flora stopped listening. This sounded just like the sort of thing Mr Burton said to APS parents in the twenty-first century – head teachers didn't seem to have changed at all.

After Peepy's speech, the lower-school choir sang "The Wild Brown Bee," and "Who is Sylvia?". And then it was their turn. Flora took a deep breath and walked out on to the stage with the others. There was a warm burst of laughter at their costumes, which made her legs feel less wobbly.

Dorothy began, in her high, clear voice:

> *"The sun was shining on the sea,*
> *Shining with all his might:*
> *He did his very best to make*
> *The billows smooth and bright."*

Flora and Pete set off on a stroll across the stage, ready to speak their lines.

> *"The Walrus and the Carpenter*
> *Were walking close at hand;*

>   They wept like anything to see
>   Such quantities of sand."

They pretended to sob – Pete was particularly good at this – and said together:

> "'If this were only cleared away,'
> They said, 'it would be grand!'
>
> 'If seven maids with seven mops
> Swept it for half a year.
> Do you suppose,' the Walrus said,
> 'That they could get it clear?'
> 'I doubt it,' said the Carpenter,
> And shed a bitter tear."

It couldn't have gone better. The girls were word perfect, the audience roared with laughter, and the applause at the end was massive. Grinning with relief and elation, Flora and Pete took off their costumes and went to sit with the other girls.

"You were wizard!" Pogo whispered, from the row behind. "Even Harbottle laughed!"

"Even DORSEY laughed!" whispered Dulcie.

Flora wished Mum and Dad could have been here. They would have been so proud, and she hadn't given them enough good reasons to be proud of her.

When I get home, she thought, *if I ever do – it's going to be so different.*

The senior-school choir sang "Jesu, Joy of Man's Desiring". Someone played a solo on the violin, and the head girl read a passage from the Bible about a virtuous woman.

After this, it was time for the awards. A little table was carried on, covered with stiff paper scrolls, and placed beside Miss Powers-Prout.

Virginia won the Classics Prize, and looked very pretty when she went up to accept it, despite the stupid white dress. Most of the awards went to the older girls, but Pogo won the History Prize, and there was a thrilling moment when Old Peepy said, "For the first time in many years, the Mrs Carstairs Cup for Sewing goes to a member of the lower school – Dulcie Latimer!"

Nobody had expected Dulcie to win anything, least of all Dulcie herself. She went up to the platform with a bright scarlet face, to accept the tiny silver cup, and the lower school broke into loud cheers that showed how popular she was. On the other side of the hall, Flora spotted Dorsey angrily wiping her eyes.

"Two awards!" Pete yelled to Flora over the din. "Our bedroom's covered with glory!"

"Lastly," said Miss Powers-Prout, "I come to the Mildred Beak Award for Excellence. Each year, this very special award goes to a girl who embodies all the fundamental values of St Winifred's – truthfulness, bravery and loyal comradeship. This year, I am delighted to give the award to Flora Fox."

A loud gasp ran through all the schoolgirls. Flora felt as if her stomach had dropped down to her knees. Suddenly everyone was looking at her, and Old Peepy was talking about her.

"A few days ago, as many of you will know, Flora's quick thinking and determination saved one of her classmates from serious injury. When she arrived at this school, some of us found her independent spirit rather startling." Several of the teachers behind her smiled at this. "True independence, however, when asserted for the benefit of the whole school, can only be a good influence. Well done, Flora – you're a credit to St Winifred's!"

Flora's head swam. The cheers were deafening, and hands were shoving her out of her seat, pushing her towards the platform. She felt awkward and embarrassed and clumsy – and incredibly proud.

Afterwards, when it was over and everyone was milling about in the hall and the dining room, she was hemmed in by girls who wanted to slap her on the back and shake her hand.

"Jolly well done, Flora!"

"Congratulations!"

Pete whispered in her ear, "I'm the only person in the world who knows how much you deserve it!"

Out in the entrance hall, under the great portrait of Dame Mildred, Lady Badger elbowed her way through the crowd, beaming all over her round face, and gave Flora a smacking kiss on the cheek.

"Well done, my dear – and you and Pete made the most hilarious Walrus and Carpenter – we laughed ourselves into fits!"

Dorsey, poker-faced as usual, said, "It was as good as the pictures."

In the middle of it all, Flora noticed something interesting about Pete. She was sparkling and laughing, bright and quick as mercury, talking her head off – nothing odd there. But she was not crowing, or swaggering, or acting as if she had been the only star of the show.

"Wasn't Flora wonderful, Mummy?" she demanded, the minute she had grabbed her parents. "I could hardly keep a straight face behind my tusks!"

Mrs Peterson shook Flora's hand. "Hello, Flora. Well done."

"Hear hear!" Mr Peterson shook her hand, and once again Flora saw that fleeting look of her own dad in twenty-first century Wimbledon. "Jolly good to see you again – Daphne's letters are absolutely full of you."

"The crowds have died down a bit round the tea tables," Pete said. "Let's go in before the cake disappears."

"Yes, let's," said her mother. "The stern gaze of Dame Mildred is making me hungry!"

"Stern?" Mr Peterson glanced up at the portrait. "I'd say she looks like rather a jolly old buzzard."

Flora looked at the portrait. For the very first time, she noticed a glint of something like humour in the painted eyes. The old buzzard was almost smiling.

19

King Cophetua and the Beggar-maid

"Have you heard about Ethel?" Bunty Hardwick pounced on the four of them, just as they were going into breakfast next morning. "It's the most fearful scandal!"

"Ethel?" Flora was anxious. "She's all right, isn't she?"

Bunty lowered her voice to a gleeful whisper. "She's getting married – to Consuela Carver's father!"

"Wh-what?"

"I swear it's true! Dimsie Scarborough told me, and she had it from one of the maids. Mr Carver's fallen madly in love with Ethel – and her mother's furious, because he's divorced and years older than her, and they're not allowed to get married in a church. But don't you think it's romantic?"

Bunty darted away to pounce on someone else with the incredible news, leaving Flora, Pete, Pogo and Dulcie in a state of shock.

"Wow," Flora said, "I forgot all about that spell – if it was because of our spell."

Pogo said, "Of course it was. What else could have done it? This thing's got magic written all over it."

Dulcie said, "It's just like *King Cophetua and the Beggar-maid* in my bedroom!"

"And their eyes met over Consuela's broken leg," Pete said thoughtfully. "Gosh, it's like a film!"

"That'll do," Miss Bradley said, suddenly swooping down on their group. "If you want to gossip, you can jolly well gossip in French!"

The compulsory French at breakfast quietened them a little, but the whole school seethed with the amazing news. Flora could sense the whispers lapping up and down the long tables like waves.

"I don't see why everyone has to act like it's some kind of disaster," she complained, once they were back upstairs making their beds. "I think it's wonderful. And it might've happened without magic – Ethel's really pretty."

Dulcie tugged at her blankets. "Doesn't she mind that Consuela's father is so OLD?"

"She's madly in love," Pete said. "Details like that don't matter when you're madly in love."

"I should think it jolly well matters to Consuela," Pogo said. "She's the most frightful snob, don't forget. Some of her snobbish friends won't want to visit her when her father's married to a servant – she might be wishing King Cophetua had stayed in Africa."

"Well, I agree with Flora and Pete," Dulcie announced. "I think it's very romantic and exactly like a fairy tale. Wasn't that a marvellous spell? Who else do we know who needs a rich husband?"

"Harbottle," suggested Pete.

They all shouted with laughter, and then had fun marrying off all the other teachers.

"Seriously," Dulcie said, "now that we know how to get rich husbands, don't we have a sort of duty to help people?"

"We should get nice rich husbands for ourselves," Pete suggested.

"It wouldn't work for us, you ass, we're only twelve," Pogo said. "And I vote we leave well alone from now on – for all we know, our spell might have ruined Consuela's life, or Ethel's. The one thing I've learned about real magic is not to mess about with it."

Had they ruined anyone's life? Flora was not sure. She couldn't exactly put it into words, but she felt there was a kind of wisdom in this force they had messed about with. Somehow, she trusted it not to do anything wrong.

And two days later, she got a chance to see the results for herself. She and Pete were running in from the garden at the end of lunch break, and there was Consuela in the hall. She sat in a big chair, one white plaster leg sticking out in front of her. Her little group of friends clustered around her. Wendy Elliot was hopping about, trying Consuela's crutches.

Consuela looked incredibly different. Flora tried to pinpoint the change. There was the plaster leg, of course, and the fact that she was wearing a very pretty pale blue dress instead of school uniform. But the main thing she looked was – happy. She was laughing, and her laughter had lost its sneer.

She glanced up at Pete and Flora, and her face reddened.

They couldn't walk away now, though Flora felt Pete would have loved to. She couldn't take her eyes off the plaster leg.

"Hello," Flora said. "How – how are you?"

"Very well, thanks."

Pete blurted out, "Does it hurt a lot?"

"Not really, if I'm careful. It's just dull having to sit all the time."

"When are you coming back to school?"

"I'm not," Consuela said. "I'm going to live in Switzerland with Daddy and – and – I expect you've heard about Ethel." She looked defiant, and her friends looked embarrassed.

Flora longed to ask what their problem was. So what if Mr Carver was divorced? And so what if he was marrying a "servant"? In the future, none of this would have mattered.

"I think it's great," she said impulsively. "Ethel's lovely."

Consuela was surprised, and a little suspicious – was Flora making fun of her?

"We all think it's incredibly romantic," she added.

This made Consuela smile. "So do I, and it all happened because of me – Ethel was such a brick when I hurt my leg. She held my hand all the time the bone was being set. Daddy said he couldn't help falling in love with her. When he told me he wanted to marry her and take us both to Switzerland, I was jolly pleased. I – I don't much like living with my mother. She's always sending me away, even in the holidays." She looked up at Flora and Pete, and the colour in her cheeks deepened. "I haven't thanked you for saving me when I broke my leg."

Pete frowned. "That's all right. I mean, you don't have to. I mean – it was mostly Flora. And I'm sorry I was beastly to you. Will you shake hands?" She held out her ink-stained hand, and the two former enemies shook hands.

If I had my phone, Flora thought, *I'd take a photo.*

"I'm glad I had a chance to say goodbye," Consuela

said. "We're leaving for London tonight."

"Give our love to Ethel," Flora said.

Consuela saw that she meant it and was not being snide, and gave her a proper, friendly smile. "Thanks, I will. I know she'll be pleased. She said if anyone asked, I was to tell them she was as happy as a princess in a fairy tale."

"Well, it is rather like a fairy tale," Wendy Elliot said. "As if someone had cast a spell!"

"Spells? Who is casting spells?" Miss Harbottle was upon them – she had a way of appearing suddenly, like a genie. "Kindly get to your classes!"

She stared at Flora, her black eyes like two specks of boiling vinegar. Flora hastily said goodbye to Consuela, and hurried away to her next lesson. When she glanced over her shoulder, Harbottle was still staring at her – staring as if she could see right through her skin to the marrow of her bones.

"Get up! Get up at once!"

Someone was calling, and light shone into her face. Flora groggily opened her eyes.

"Hurry up! I haven't got all night!"

Harbottle had snapped on all the lamps and stood in the middle of the bedroom floor. The long sleeves of her shabby black gown looked like the folded wings of a bird of prey. Flora sat up in bed, her heart drumming. What was going on? This was not a dream. Pete, Pogo and Dulcie were sitting up in their beds, too shocked and sleepy to do anything but gape.

"I want the book," Harbottle said. "I know you've got it. Give it to me at once."

The girls all looked at each other in astonishment.

"Yes!" Harbottle snapped. "I mean THAT book – the volume with which you have been playing your foolish games. Please don't try to deny it. The book happens to be my property."

"We thought it belonged to Dame Mildred Beak," Flora said.

"She left it to me in her will – does that satisfy your legal mind, Miss Fox? Good gracious, child, this is no time to argue! In the wrong hands, that book is more dangerous than a loaded gun!"

They all looked at each other again. The game was well and truly up. Pogo got out of bed and knelt on the floor to pull up the loose board. She took out the battered old book of spells and Dame Mildred's notebook, and handed them both to Miss Harbottle.

"This, too!" Harbottle peered at the notebook. "Dear me, I haven't seen this for years! It's my fault, I suppose. I ought to have known." She was talking to herself. "Someone was always going to find them. She warned me! Why didn't I listen? Who can calculate the harm that might have been done?" She glanced up sharply, at the pale faces of the girls. "Put on your dressing gowns and slippers, switch off your lamps and come to my study."

They obeyed her in silence. It was known all over the school that no girl or teacher had ever been inside Harbottle's study. Ethel had told them that only the oldest of the maids was allowed inside to clean it. Flora had stopped being scared, and felt herself getting incredibly curious. What could the old bat be hiding in there? She wouldn't put anything past her.

Miss Harbottle's study was across a landing at the very end of the bedroom corridor. She jerked open the door, and the four girls walked into a cave of jumbled shadows — Flora's first impression was that Harbottle lived inside a junk shop. As her eyes got used to the shadows, she saw that the room was stuffed with things. The walls were covered with books, and there were heaps of books all over the floor. There were also glass cases of fossils, and a dusty Roman head with no nose. The only light came from one lamp on the desk, and its reflection in the big mirror over the fireplace. Though it was summer, a small coal fire burned in the grate. Flora was hot in her dressing gown.

Harbottle stood behind her desk, and the four girls lined up in front of it — Pete managed to knock over a pile of books. She turned bright red, but Miss Harbottle did not seem to have noticed. She was looking hard at Flora.

"You were summoned from the future, weren't you?"

She knew.

Flora shivered. Somehow, the fact that Harbottle knew her secret made it more real, and less like a game. "Yes," she said quietly.

"What a blind old fool I've been! I know the look of a person who has been summoned," Harbottle went on, "and I knew there was something odd about you – I simply didn't put two and two together. I should've had my suspicions when you predicted another world war and wrote that essay about the next century, but I didn't think about magic until the business with Ethel – the Elliot gel babbling about spells – then it all fell into place. You'd better tell me what other spells you've been mucking about with."

Pete said, "Ethel was the last one. And before that, Flora's summoning was our only bullseye."

"Thank you, Daphne," Harbottle said. "That is a great relief. I'm not going to punish any of you – though you richly deserve it – because it's partly my fault."

"Your fault?" Flora didn't understand.

"When Mildred Beak died," Harbottle said slowly, "she made me promise to burn all her father's books about magic. I was surprised – I thought she'd destroyed them years ago, after the rather disturbing success of our early experiments."

She paused, as she did in class when she was waiting for an answer.

Flora was puzzled. She didn't see how Harbottle could have done any "experiments" with Dame Mildred Beak. Harbottle was ancient, but surely not old enough to have known the old sorceress.

"Of course!" Pogo cried out suddenly. "I know who you are – you're Celeste!"

Harbottle's thin lips puckered into a smile. "Yes, I'm Celeste. You read about me in this notebook, I dare say."

It took a second for Flora to remember that Celeste was the girl in Dame Mildred Beak's diary – the one who let Miss Beak do the summoning spell on her because she wanted to stay at school. This was incredible. She stared into Harbottle's wrinkled old face, searching for the unhappy, motherless girl in the diary. She had wondered what happened to Celeste, and she'd been under their noses the whole time. How had she turned into Horrible Harbottle? Perhaps she wasn't so horrible after all – when you looked really closely, you could see how she must have been when her fuzz of hair was black instead of white.

"Miss Beak was a true mother to me," Harbottle said. "I shouldn't have broken my promise to her – but when it came to the point, I couldn't bear to burn valuable old books, and I had them bricked up in the attic room. I should have known one of you little monkeys would think of climbing in through the window! Heh heh! I was just such a monkey myself, when I was a gel." She let out another grating chuckle. "Well, I've learned my lesson. The bricks are coming down and those books are going on the nearest fire. And you'd better forget about magic as fast as possible. I know that's hard when Flora is here – but I have a feeling she won't be here much longer."

She smiled at Flora, and Flora's heart leapt with hope. Suddenly, she wanted her real home so intensely that she could hardly bear it.

"You three gels from the present," Harbottle said, "may go back to bed. Miss Fox, you will stay here."

Afterwards, when she tried to remember the midnight hour she spent alone with Harbottle, Flora was not sure how much of it she had dreamed. Once Pete, Pogo and Dulcie had gone, the scary old barnacle sat Flora down in a soft armchair beside the fire, and made her a delicious cup of sugary cocoa. Harbottle herself had a glass of sherry, from a bottle she kept in her desk. It was as if she had declared a truce in the eternal war between girls and teachers. Sipping her drink, she asked all sorts of questions about the future.

Flora answered as well as she could. It was not easy, because Harbottle kept asking about politics, and international relations, and people she had never heard of.

"Oh well," Harbottle said, "you can't be expected to know about the next Archbishop of Canterbury. Just tell me anything you can remember."

Flora told her about the war and the first landing on the moon. She was pretty sure there had been a woman prime minister before she was born – Harbottle was particularly fascinated by this. She did her best to describe twenty-first century things, though she couldn't find the right words, and they sounded rather silly in 1930s language.

But she needn't have worried. Harbottle loved it all. "I do wish I could live to see – what did you call them? Knee-tops?"

"Laptops." Flora was so relaxed that she smiled at this. Somehow, half hidden in the shadows, Harbottle no longer seemed ancient. It was almost like talking to another girl. It was almost like travelling back in time and talking to Celeste. Suddenly, she knew exactly what the schoolgirl Celeste had been like, and wondered if you could unlock all old people to find the young selves they had hidden away. *I wish I'd tried that with Granny*, she thought. *I never made any effort to know her.*

"My guess," Celeste Harbottle said, "is that you'll go home when you have finished turning Daphne

Peterson into a decent sort. There is already a vast improvement."

Impulsively, Flora said, "I wish I could do something for Virginia."

"Virginia Denning? What's the matter with her?"

"I don't want her to go back to Vienna."

"Why? Is it about to be destroyed by an earthquake?"

"I don't really know. I just have a really bad feeling about it," Flora said. "I sort of remember that something terrible is going to happen to Jewish people."

Harbottle's eyebrows went up. "Jews? Why?"

"I don't know!" Flora had the sick feeling of dread again. "Look, Miss Harbottle — before you burn the magic books, couldn't you do something to keep her here?"

"Hmm." The wrinkled tortoise face was thoughtful. "You're not afraid of asking difficult questions. As a matter of fact — and I trust you never to breathe a word of this — I do still perform the occasional small spell. I studied Miss Beak's books in secret, and made my own notes."

Wow, Flora thought, *she looks like a witch because she IS a witch.*

"I'd better burn those, too — it would be a fine thing if I dropped dead suddenly, and some nosy gel found them." The old witch sighed. "But I'll see what I can do

242

about Virginia. Have you any other requests?"

She looked so friendly that Flora felt brave. "Yes, but it's not about magic. I've taken the place of another Flora Fox, and when we swap back – you see, she's been in a very modern school in the next century—"

"And you want me to go easy on her."

This made Flora smile. "She's probably picked up a few modern habits you won't like much. And I think she seems quite cool – nice, I mean. Her memories are nice."

Harbottle chuckled. "Poor child, she'll be starting another new school back in the Dark Ages, with not a knee-top or ear-pod in sight!"

Flora spluttered on the last sip of cocoa. "What I mean is, could you give her a bit of time to get used to being back in the past?"

"Very well, I'll make a few allowances." Harbottle swigged the last of her sherry and poured herself a little more. "Here, I'll show you something. Stand up, and go to the mantelpiece."

Flora went to the mantelpiece beside the hot fire, and watched Harbottle curiously. Her brisk little claws dug in the drawers of her desk, pulling out a number of small, dusty bottles. She set these in a row and produced a small brown bowl.

"Earthenware," she said. "Nothing else works as a conductor." Even when she was dabbling in magic, she couldn't stop being a teacher. One by one, she took the stoppers off the bottles and put a pinch on whatever was inside into the bowl. "These are herbs – common garden herbs – that must be dried and preserved in a particular way. Look into the mirror over the mantelpiece."

Flora turned to face the big mirror.

"What do you see?"

"Your study. You. Me."

"Keep looking at your reflection." Harbottle muttered something – Flora thought she heard Latin – picked up the bowl, and threw the herbs on to the glowing red coals.

There was a strong, musty smell, like a cupboard nobody has opened for years. The mirror misted over.

"Keep looking!"

The mist cleared. Flora cried out in amazement. The reflection in the mirror showed a different room, and the face of a different girl.

"Now what do you see?"

"I – I—" She couldn't reply. The girl in the mirror stared back at her in equal amazement. It was Flora's own face – sort of. But this girl's brown hair had blonde streaks, and she was wearing eye make-up and gold earrings. Flora knew those earrings. Mum and Dad had given them to her for her last birthday. "It's the other Flora!"

Across the yawning gulf of years, the two Floras stared at each other. At this very moment, far away in the future, the other Flora stood before a mirror in Penrice Hall, gazing into the distant past.

"Yes, I see her," Harbottle said, "but only just – it's still misty. Can you see the room behind her?"

The two Floras had been staring into each other's faces. "Yes."

"Your vision is clearer than mine. Please describe it."

Flora looked behind the other Flora and saw a small bedroom, with purple walls that were covered with posters. "I can see a desk – and that's my laptop! And my hoodie – one of my shoes – my big jar of Pampering Body Cream." It was odd to see all her stuff.

"She can't hear you, I'm afraid," Harbottle said.

This was frustrating, when there were so many things Flora wanted to say. The two girls smiled at each other. Flora mouthed, "Hello."

The other Flora mouthed, "Hi!" She lifted her hand and put it against the mirror. Her palm was flat and white, as if the mirror was a window. Flora put her own palm against it. The glass was cold, yet she thought she felt a kind of warmth passing between them.

The vision lasted for about five minutes. The mist rose up again, and when it faded, the reflection in the mirror had changed back to Harbottle's cluttered study. Flora was touching hands with her own reflection, and

Harbottle stood behind her.

They were both quiet, stunned by what they had seen. The brass clock on the mantelpiece whirred loudly, and let out a single chime.

"One o'clock – you'd better go back to bed." Harbottle seemed to shake herself awake. "Please don't talk about any of this – not even to the girls in your dorm. Once you are called back, they will forget a great deal."

"I hope they don't forget me," Flora said wistfully, thinking how much she would miss her three friends.

Harbottle patted her shoulder, with surprising gentleness. "Oh, they won't forget you. True friendship is stronger than the strongest magic. Sleep well, future-girl."

20
The Ten-Bob Note

On the last morning of term, Flora knew before she opened her eyes that something was different. The air was tugging at her – that was the only way she could describe it. It was like being sucked in by a very gentle vacuum cleaner. The past was as solid as ever, but she could hear a very, very faint background murmur that might have been the roar of all the mixed noises of the future.

Home.

For the very first time since her arrival at St Winifred's, she had a powerful sense that her real home was nearby, as if the space between past and future had narrowed.

Her own calmness surprised her. She didn't say

anything to Pete, Pogo and Dulcie until after breakfast, when they all went back to the bedroom to strip their beds and finish packing. "I can't describe the feeling, or explain it. I just know I'm going home – my real home, in the future."

"Well, I can't say I'm surprised," Pogo said. "We thought the magic might be waiting till the end of term. Do you know when it's going to happen?"

"No. I don't really know anything. It's just a feeling."

The others were silent. It was a shock to remember, in the turmoil of the last day, that Flora did not belong to their world.

Dulcie said, "I was hoping you'd come back next term. I suppose that'll be the other Flora."

"I can't wait to ask her what she got up to in the twenty-first century," Pogo said, "but I'll miss you. You've been an asset to this bedroom."

"Hear hear!" Dulcie said.

Pete sat on the edge of her bed, her head hanging forlornly, and said nothing.

There was another silence. Today, the four of them were going in four different directions. Flora was to take the train to London, where a Mrs Markham, who was the other Flora's aunt, would meet her at Paddington. Pogo was off to Birmingham, to stay at her uncle's vicarage with all her brothers and two girl cousins. Dulcie was going home to Merrythorpe, and

Pete's parents were coming to pick her up on their way to Scotland.

Dulcie's lower lip trembled. "We won't ever see you again. When you get home to the future, we'll all be so old that we're dead!" A tear rolled down her cheek.

"If you're still alive," Flora said, "I'll look you up."

Pete raised her head. "Do you promise?"

"OK – if I can find you. I'll do my best."

"How funny," Pete said. "You'll be just as you are now, but I'll be as old as Harbottle."

This was a very weird thought. By the time Flora saw her three friends again – if she ever did – they would have done years and years of living. She wished she knew what would happen to them all, especially Pete. She was sure Pete's life would be interesting.

Pete said, "You might not recognize me." An idea lit up her face – you could always tell when Pete had an idea. She dived to open her overnight bag and took out her purse. From this, she took a ten-shilling note.

Pogo whistled. "Ten shillings! You've still got ten shillings at the end of term!" This was worth fifty pence in Flora's time, which wasn't such a big deal, but in 1935 it was a small fortune.

"My people like me to have plenty of money, in case of emergencies. And this is an emergency." Pete tore the note in half – Dulcie let out a squeak of horror. "I'll keep one half of this," she said, "and Flora, you take the other half. Then you'll know who I am when we meet again. Even if I look like Harbottle."

"A typically melodramatic gesture," Pogo said. "What if Flora can't take her half to the future? Ten bob wasted!"

"I'll still have my half," Pete said impatiently. "I'll always keep it, and that way I'll always remember you. And I promise I'll start looking for you as soon as you're born. I'll do my best not to die before then." She pushed one half of the ten-shilling note into Flora's hand.

"I'll never forget you – any of you." Flora looked at Pete, the person she would miss most. The others were lovely, but Pete was more. She was as quick and brilliant as a kingfisher, with a huge appetite for living and laughing and throwing herself at new things, and Wimbledon would seem very flat without her. "Thanks for being so nice to me, and I'm sorry I was a bit of a pain at first."

"Yes, you were," Pete said, grinning, "but not as painful as I was."

"You'll miss Neville marrying Virginia," Dulcie said. "There's no need to pinch me, Pogo Lawrence – we all know they're madly in love. Virginia never stops reading his letters."

"Can't you think about anything else? Too much romance isn't good for a brain like yours." Pogo picked up her overnight bag. "We'd better go downstairs. It was fascinating to meet you, Flora. The other Flora might turn out to be perfectly nice – but you'll always be the fourth musketeer."

"Thanks." Flora's eyes prickled with tears. She would miss Pogo's dry humour and sharp mind. "Say hi to Neville – and maybe drop a hint that Stalin isn't as wonderful as he thinks." Suddenly, scraps of the future were rushing back to her like pieces of a jigsaw. "I've just remembered that my dad has a dartboard with Stalin's face on. I don't think anyone likes him any more."

Pogo was startled. "Are you sure? Well, I'll try. But I'm afraid he won't listen."

"And Dulcie – give my love to Lady B. and Dorsey." She'd miss Dulcie, too. It would be oddly lonely, falling asleep without Dulcie and Mr Bunny a few feet away in the next bed.

"I will." Dulcie hesitated for a moment, then flung her arms around Flora and hugged her hard.

Pogo put down her bag. "For once, I think a group hug is called for."

The four of them hugged.

Pete squeezed Flora's hand, the one clutching her half of the ten-shilling note, and whispered, "Remember!"

There were twenty-three girls on the train to London,

251

under the easy-going guardianship of Miss Bradley. They were all wildly excited, chattering like starlings. In Flora's compartment, Dorothy Sykes passed round a bag of sweets – bullseyes, which Flora didn't like because they tasted of cloves and stung your tongue. She took one absent-mindedly. It sat in her cheek, cold as a pebble. When was she going home? Was it possible to swap bodies with the other Flora without anyone noticing? Her half of the ten-shilling note was still scrunched in her hand. She had managed not to let go of it while getting on the train. She was hoping that if she held it tightly in her hand, she could take it back to her own time.

I'm going to start searching for Pete the second I get home, she thought. *I don't care how old she is.*

Virginia, sitting beside her, nudged her gently. "Are you all right? You're awfully quiet."

"I'm fine." Flora couldn't tell her about the murmur of the crowd inside her head, still very distant but getting closer. "I didn't like saying goodbye to my friends, that's all."

"You'll see them again in a few weeks," Virginia said. "Perhaps you're not looking forward to the hols. Where will you be staying?"

Flora had to concentrate hard to get into the other Flora's mind. "At my Aunt Mary's. I haven't seen her since I was little."

"Rather daunting for you, I should think."

"She – she's very nice." The other Flora was moving away, and Flora thought she'd better change the subject before she had to answer any more questions. "What about you? Are you going straight to Vienna?"

"No," Virginia was smiling. "I'm going straight to London, to stay with my glamorous cousin until my parents join me. Rather a curious thing happened – my father was suddenly offered a professorship at the LSE, and my parents are moving to London. Isn't that wonderful?"

"Oh – that's so cool!" Flora felt like cheering – good old Harbottle must've kept her promise and cast one more spell. Now that she knew Virginia was safe, she could leave the past with a lighter heart.

If she ever did leave. The train rattled on, and the unpleasant boiled sweet in Flora's mouth got smaller and smaller, and still the past gripped her and refused to let her go. They stopped at a station, where several girls left the train.

Suddenly, Flora was desperately tired. She yawned and shut her eyes.

"Flora? What's the matter, dear?"

Miss Bradley's voice was swept away by the roar of all the other sounds – crowds, explosions, snatches of music, whirling round her until her head swam. A scream tore out of her. She was a bullet, shooting

253

forward faster than the speed of light. She felt herself somersaulting through the empty air and landing neatly in her own body.

The roar stopped, as if switched off. Flora heard only the brisk rattle of a train. She could no longer feel her tight collar or troublesome suspenders. Her school uniform had gone, and she was wearing something light and comfortable. She dared to open her eyes, and saw her own jeans and trainers. Her iPod was on the little table in front of her.

Oh, joy-joy-joy, she was back. She was about to see Mum and Dad – she could call them and hear their voices right now! There was such a lot she had to tell them – so many questions she needed to ask. Had they guessed the other Flora was not their real daughter? Had they missed her?

Her left hand was still clenched into a fist. She uncurled her fingers and found her half of Pete's ten-shilling note. It was incredible to think that it had been given to her that morning, more than seventy years ago. Had Pete kept her half? It was yet more incredible, and rather sad, to think that the quicksilver girl who had given her the note no longer existed. She had turned into an old woman, if she was still alive. Flora found her pink purse in the front pocket of her backpack and put the note away carefully.

Something bleeped in her jeans pocket. Flora nearly jumped out of her skin. Of course – her phone. Someone had sent her a text. She dug into her pocket, and her phone fitted into her palm as if she had never been away. She'd been worried about forgetting the twenty-first-century world, but found she was slipping back as easily as a duck slipping into a pond. The text was from Mum. "Dad meeting you – can't wait to CU at home!!xxxx"

Flora was glad the modern, open-plan carriage was empty. She was shaking so much, she was sure she looked crazy. Mum was waiting for her, with not a clue that her child had nearly been lost to her for ever. Her fingers trembling – crikey, the buttons on this phone were tiny – she called Mum.

"Hi, Flora!"

"Hi, Mum." Flora had to make an effort not to burst into babyish tears at the sound of her voice.

"Did you get my text? Dad will be at the station to meet you – I'm staying here with Granny. We're both dying to show off the new flat." (Flora had almost forgotten about the new granny flat in the Wimbledon garage.) "It's absolutely lovely – what?" A voice said something in the background. "Sorry? You want me to say what?" There was a pause. Mum laughed. "Granny wants me to give you a message. I haven't a clue what she's talking about, but she wants you to know that she looks nothing like Harbottle. OK?"

Flora gasped, "Harbottle?"

"That's it – she says you'll understand. See you soon, darling – bye!"

"Bye." Flora sat very still for a few minutes, gaping stupidly at the phone in her hand.

How did Granny know about Harbottle?

Something very odd was happening inside her head. Her brain was a kaleidoscope, at the moment the pieces fall into a new pattern. The other Flora had gone, and without the clutter of her memories, everything was suddenly clear.

Of course! She almost laughed aloud. What an idiot she had been. There had been endless clues – the fact that Pete's middle name was Flora, the dream about Granny in school uniform, the way Mr Peterson had reminded her of Dad, the snooty look Pete got when she was being stubborn – and she hadn't suspected a thing.

What was it the portrait of Mildred Beak had said in the dream? "*If you two cannot be friends, you will never know.*" She knew now, and the truth took her breath away.

21

The Four Musketeers

ete was – Granny. She had been at school with her own grandmother.

"Crikey!" Flora whispered. The electrifying Pete and her crabby old granny were one and the same person. It was all obvious now. That magic – or whatever you called it – was incredibly clever. It had sent Flora to save Pete from the awful consequences of pushing Consuela into the quarry, and to stop her growing up into a mean old bag. It was a bit of a shame that the magic couldn't have kept the two girls away from the quarry in the first place, but Consuela had done pretty well out of her broken leg, and perhaps that was part of the whole picture.

The trolley came. Flora treated herself to the modern

luxuries of Coke and crisps (which tasted gorgeous) and tried to think calmly.

There were no more closed doors in her memory. She remembered now why she had been so anxious about Virginia. Millions of Jewish people had been murdered by the Nazis during the Second World War. They'd had a special assembly at APS, when a lady who had been in a concentration camp came to talk to the school about the Holocaust. If Virginia had been in Vienna, she would have been sent off to a gas chamber. The thought turned Flora ice cold. If only she'd been able to remember all this in 1935, she could have done more – she could have run away from St Winifred's, somehow got to Holland, found Anne Frank, begged her to move to England – but that had not been allowed. And it probably wouldn't have been possible, anyway. The magic only let you take on what you could handle.

She looked out of the window. The train had sliced through the suburbs, and was slowing down as it entered the centre of London. At Paddington, Flora gathered up all her stuff – so light and colourful after the leather cases she had hefted this morning in 1935 – and her heart leapt when she saw Dad waiting on the platform. He was sleek and smiling, and far more relaxed than the unshaven nervous wreck she had left behind all those months ago. She scrambled off the train, threw herself at him and hugged him fiercely.

"Well, let's look at you," Dad said. "The webcam pictures didn't really do you justice. I'd swear you're taller – and have you got thinner? Mum's at home with Granny."

"And is Granny – you know—" Flora hesitated, wondering how to ask if she had got any nicer. Dad wouldn't know what she was talking about. As far as he was concerned, nothing had changed.

Dad gave her arm a reassuring squeeze. "Don't worry, darling. The operation was a great success – she's thrown away the crutches, and just uses a walking stick now."

Flora had been so busy thinking about the old Pete – the one she had seen this morning – that she'd forgotten about the broken hip. It was awful to think of live-wire Pete as an infirm old lady.

"I know you hated leaving her," Dad said, picking up her laptop case. "We did feel bad about sending you away, when you wanted so much to be with her. I'm glad you ended up liking Penrice Hall."

"It was great – sorry I made such a fuss." Here was another change. Dad was talking about a new, improved Flora, who had only protested about boarding school because she wanted to stay with her beloved grandmother.

"Oh, you were all right," Dad said. "Your grandmother was the one who had us running round in circles. You'll be happy to hear that I persuaded her not to sell the Casa Boffi. Now she's talking about leaving it to you in her will."

"Me?"

"She says you're the only one with enough artistic temperament to appreciate it properly – Flora? Are you all right, darling?"

"I'm great." Flora decided she had better keep the amazement out of her face as much as possible. Everything was amazing. Apparently, she and Granny were now the best of friends – just as she and Pete had been. For the first time, she began to feel excited about seeing Pete again. "It's just sort of weird to be back in London."

She had forgotten how many cars there were in the twenty-first century. Dad's Volvo was parked in a street near the station, where there seemed to be more cars than buildings. It unlocked with a beep when he pressed his key. Modern life was fast, and noisy, and crowded. The inside of the car smelled of chemicals and sun-baked plastic. Outside, the pavements swarmed with people who wore no hats and hardly any clothes. It was bewildering, and wonderful.

On the way home, while Flora gazed out of the window drinking in all the movement and energy and bright colours, Dad talked cheerfully about moving Granny into her new flat. "You won't be surprised to

260

hear that she's bought herself a gigantic television. Did you watch much TV at school?"

Flora said, "Not really. There was too much to do."

"I must say, darling, I'm thrilled that you involved yourself in so many activities while you were at Penrice. Jeff said that once you got over your initial shyness, you made a fantastic contribution." Dad chuckled. "I do wish we'd been able to come to the end-of-term concert – I'd love to have seen your famous comedy striptease!"

Flora squeaked, and turned it into a cough. Striptease? The other Flora had certainly come out of her shell at Penrice Hall. She'd have to get back into it pretty quickly if she wanted to fit in at St Win's.

Mum came out to the front gate as soon as she heard the car. She was smiling, and how trim and pretty she looked, compared with the shapeless, hairy teachers at St Winifred's. Flora hugged her. It was wizard – brilliant – to be back, but she couldn't think about anything except Pete. When had she guessed that her granddaughter was the Flora from her school? Had she always known?

The door that had once led to the garage was now the door to the new granny flat.

"You go in," Mum said. "I'll bring you something to drink in a minute, but I'm in the middle of putting things on plates. Granny's invited a couple of friends to tea."

"Friends?"

"One of them is Baroness Hooper, no less. Do go in, darling – she's been on tenterhooks all day."

"OK – I just have to get something from my purse." Flora took out her half of the ten-shilling note, and scrunched it in the palm of her hand. It all seemed so far-fetched that she was already scared of looking silly. She knocked on the door.

"Is that Flora? Come in!" It was a deep, cracked old voice, not at all like Pete's. She pushed open the door.

The new room had long windows that opened on to the garden. It was filled with furniture, pictures and books from the house in Italy.

Granny sat beside the new window, in an old person's armchair with a high back, with her walking stick hooked over one of the arms. She was just the same. Her hair was white, her nose was a long beak and her face was covered with wrinkles.

"Flora."

"Hello." Flora wasn't sure what to call her. Her message about Harbottle showed that Granny knew – but she couldn't see any sign of Pete.

Granny was clutching a battered leather folder stuffed with pieces of paper. She opened it and reached into an inner pocket. Her fingers were long and thin, and her diamond ring was loose between her joints. She held out what looked like a limp, tattered, dirty scrap of paper.

"I never lost it," Granny said. "Somehow, I've managed to hold on to it through all my travels."

It was the other half of the ten-shilling note. Her grandmother's face creased into a gleeful smile.

Flora cried, "Pete?"

And Pete said, "Isn't this a hoot?"

"This is probably stranger for you than it is for me," Pete said. "When you saw me this morning, I was twelve."

Flora giggled. "Do you remember this morning?"

"I do, as a matter of fact." Granny raised her eyebrows haughtily, looking exactly like the old Pete. "You promised to find me in the future – even if I looked like Miss Harbottle."

This made them both laugh. The more Flora talked to her grandmother, the more clearly Pete shone out of her. "The magic happened when I was on the train," she said.

"I know. It created quite a sensation at the time. That jolly teacher told me all about it, the one with the thick ankles. What was her name?"

"Miss Bradley."

"Yes, of course. Miss Bradley. I wonder what happened to her?" Pete broke off to sigh. "Anyway, apparently you turned white as a sheet and fainted."

"Wow!" Flora was glad she had missed this drama.

"And when you woke up, you apparently looked at your clothes as if you'd never seen them before – and then you said something that sounded like 'Krupp! I've come back!' The other Flora didn't live it down for ages."

They were laughing again, though Flora couldn't help feeling sorry for the other Flora, tasting the delights of the future only to have them snatched away.

She sipped her tea – which was, surprisingly, what she had wanted when Mum offered to make her a drink. She'd got fond of tea at St Winifred's, and modern tea was about a thousand times nicer. She decided she liked the new room. There was, as Dad had said, a vast television set. Granny/Pete knew how to make herself comfortable. And she was still untidy – for someone who could only hobble a few steps, she had made a lot of mess. Her sofa was heaped with newspapers, and there were loose sweets scattered on the carpet. Flora picked these up, and put them back in the large tin of Celebrations on the table beside Pete's chair.

She asked, "When did it hit you that I was the Flora Fox from school?"

Pete sighed. "You're going to think I'm an awful fool, but I didn't work it out until about a month ago."

"A month! What about when I was born?"

Pete sighed again. "I was in another country. When your father told me about his baby daughter, and said

264

he was naming you Flora, I might have remembered that there was a Flora Fox at my school. But I'd lost touch with her. It was such a long, long time ago – one forgets so much."

"You can't have forgotten the magic!"

"It's funny," Pete mused, "we did sort of forget it. We got used to the other Flora awfully quickly. She didn't even look exactly like you, and we were the only people who noticed. We asked her about the future – and she talked about it a lot at first. But then we all sort of moved on. We were growing up, and there were other things to think about. In my case, I'm sorry to say, the opposite sex." She did not look sorry. "Anyway, I got my first inkling when I heard your parents talking about Penrice Hall. I knew I'd heard the name before, but I couldn't for the life of me remember where. And then, while I was coming round after my operation, I had the most extraordinary dream. I was back at school, in the hall, and in came Flora Fox from my dorm – only it was you."

"And Mildred Beak spoke to you!" Flora cried excitedly. "I had the same dream – exactly the same! She wanted us to be friends!"

Pete smiled. "She did, didn't she? I wanted it too. I didn't get enough of you when you were little – to tell the truth, I'm not very good with babies and small children. But I saw what I'd done wrong when you came to Italy. I should have made more effort to know you."

Flora said, "That's what I thought about you. I'm sorry I was such a pig."

"You weren't that bad."

"Yes, I was. I was mean to Ella, and she hasn't spoken to me since."

"Oh dear," Pete said, "I suspect that was partly my fault. See if you can invite her round here for tea or something, and we'll all start again."

"She might not want to come, even if I say sorry."

"Oh, I'll telephone her mother and force her to come," Pete said cheerfully. "When you're very old and slightly famous, it's quite easy to make people do things."

It would be brilliant to repair the friendship with Ella, and for the first time, Flora saw that it might be possible – not because Pete/Granny was "slightly famous", but because she now knew what kind of apology was due. "That would be great – as long as you don't say she's lumpy again."

"Did I say that?"

"And you said I was a little weasel."

"Did I? I'm dreadfully sorry. I promise that when Ella comes, I'll be on my very best behaviour." Pete's shaky hand reached out to touch Flora's. It felt like metal covered with silk. "I might have forgotten the details, but I never forgot to be grateful to you. Thanks to you I learned to think about other people's feelings. And to control my temper – which is useful when one is constantly getting divorced. Nothing could stop me pushing that child into the quarry – more's the pity – but at least you managed to stop me leaving her there for hours and hours. I often thought about it afterwards, and how different everything would have been for me if she'd been more seriously hurt and everyone found out what I'd done. Thank you, Flora."

Flora was embarrassed. She moved her hand away from her grandmother's to take another sweet from the tin. "You were quite good for me too. When I arrived at St Win's, I was pretty much as spoiled as you were. You called me Princess Flora. And you said you'd throw me out of the window if I didn't stop going on about my shower room."

Pete gave a hoot of laughter. "Oh, Lord, your en suite shower room! How could I have forgotten that? We thought you were telling stories."

They both giggled again, just as they had done this very morning, and Flora could suddenly see the old Pete glowing through the baggy, wrinkled skin of the new one. She was the old Pete, trapped in a body that had become a cage. It was painful to think of Pete being so near the end of her life, when she needed her to live for ever. "Does your hip hurt much?"

"Only when I laugh or fart," her grandmother said, with a wicked look that was totally Pete-like. "Don't worry, darling. As I keep telling your poor father, I'll be fine as long as I don't skid on any more grapes."

A black taxi drew up in the street outside. Pete glanced out of the window. "Ah, my friends are here. I wanted to mark your homecoming with a tea party. I started planning it as soon as I remembered you were Flora from school."

Flora looked out of the window and saw the taxi driver helping a wobbly old lady out of his cab. Another old lady struggled out behind her.

"My dear old chums, Mrs Enderby and Baroness Hooper." Pete was laughing at her. "Oh, Flora, can't you guess? You last saw them this morning!"

"What? You don't mean – Pogo and Dulcie?"

Pete was very pleased with herself. "I told them! I told them you were Flora the future-girl! Dulcie was thrilled, but Pogo was sceptical – she might take a little convincing. She hasn't changed!"

Flora's head was swimming again. Pete had been enough of a shock. Now she was listening to the arrival of two more ancient twelve-year-olds.

Mum showed in the visitors. She was rather shy and extremely polite. "Flora, this is Mrs Enderby. And this is Baroness Hooper – you might have seen her on the news – anyway, I'll fetch some tea."

"Yes, please," said Mrs Enderby.

Mum raised her eyebrows at Flora, who quickly pushed the nearest chair towards her. Mrs Enderby looked like an inflatable fat person who has had half the air let out. She sat down with an "Ooof!"

"Thank you, that would be lovely," said Baroness Hooper. She was small and spry, and pulled up her own chair.

Flora stared at the two of them, searching for the girls she had hugged goodbye that morning. Mrs Enderby, when you looked over the stack of chins, was a lot like Lady Badger. But she still radiated an air of innocent kindness and slight daftness that was totally Dulcie. And she stared back at Flora in a typically Dulcie-ish way. As for wiry, wrinkled little Baroness Hooper, she was more like Pogo every minute – Flora would have known those shrewd eyes anywhere.

The moment Mum closed the door behind her, Flora burst out, "Pogo – Dulcie?"

"Good grief," said Baroness Hooper, "nobody's called me Pogo for years! I'll be perfectly honest, when Pete phoned me and started going on about magic, I thought she'd finally lost her remaining marbles."

"Oh, charming!" Pete said. "Can't you see I'm right? Don't you remember?"

Pogo suddenly grinned at Flora. "Yes, I can see it now. It's all rushing back to me. I somehow managed to

269

persuade myself that the magic business had only been a game. Hello, Flora."

Dulcie leaned towards Flora. "I knew you at once. How priceless that you shared a dorm with your own grandmother!"

"And the awful little Fox boy, who bothered me at Sheringham, was your grandfather," Pete said. "I'm glad to think you met my dear old parents that time – well, your great-grandparents, of course."

"I found myself remembering all sorts of things about school," Dulcie said. "Those vast knickers they used to make us wear! I described them to my granddaughter the other day, and she absolutely howled with laughter."

Flora had a sudden mental picture of Dulcie as she had seen her that morning, standing in her vest and knickers while she carefully stowed her rabbit in her overnight bag, saying, "In you go, Mr Bunny!" and giving him an entirely serious kiss. It was enormously odd to think of her with a granddaughter.

"I remembered the toad-in-the-hole we had on Sundays," Pogo said. "And the Army and Navy biscuits in my tuck box. And did we really crawl along a gutter, or did I make that up?"

"No, you didn't," Flora said. "And you didn't imagine the magic – none of it. Remember the spell we did for Ethel?"

To her disappointment, the three old ladies looked blank.

"Ethel – you know – who bought us illegal sweets!"

"Of course!" cried Dulcie. "She married King Cophetua – the Carver's father! Come on, of course you remember!"

"I saw her again," Pete said, "in Monte Carlo, after the war. She was as pretty as ever, and had a string of little Carvers. I do hope her mother forgave her for not getting married in church."

Flora asked, "What about Neville? Did he marry Virginia?"

Her three old friends were silent for a moment.

Pogo said, "You don't know – why should you? Neville died in 1936, in the Spanish Civil War."

"Oh." Flora had been prepared to hear that Neville had died as an old man. It was a shock to know that it had happened the year after she met him.

"He went to Spain to fight the fascists," Pogo said, with the remnants of her old pride in him. "He was shot by a sniper, while trying to help the wounded."

"Oh." Flora could see him in her mind, as she had seen him only a couple of months ago, laughing and vigorous, throwing sticks into the sea for the dogs. Tears rushed to her eyes.

"My dear," Pogo said, her voice gentle, "I didn't mean to make you cry."

"Sorry."

"No, you mustn't be sorry. It's ancient history to me, but I can't help being glad there's someone left to cry for him. Good old Nev!"

Dulcie said, "You did enough crying at the time. I remember how awful it was when the telegram came."

Pogo sighed. "Old Peepy was very decent. She told me I should be proud of him, because he died for his principles."

"How did Virginia take it?" Flora asked.

"Oh, poor thing, she was quite broken-hearted! But she got over it, because people do, and she ended up marrying someone in the Foreign Office."

The door opened. Mum came in with a tray of tea and biscuits. Flora hastily wiped her eyes, so her mother wouldn't see that she'd been crying. When the four of them were alone again, Pogo changed the subject by giving Flora a brief history of her career. She had gone to Cambridge, and then to the Houses of Parliament, where she had been a Labour MP. She was now a baroness and worked in the House of Lords, which she said was quite a lot like school.

"And in between all that, I found the time to get married and have three children."

"I just got married," Dulcie said happily, her mouth full of chocolate biscuit. "I'm sure you're not at all surprised to hear that – you remember how thick I was at St Win's. I spent the last year of the war working as a Land Girl on a farm in Gloucestershire, and married the farmer. We had five children." She added, "We only meant to have three – the twins were a mistake." This was such a Dulcie-ish comment that they all burst out laughing again.

The old ladies mostly wanted to ask Flora questions about their old school.

"Didn't Mademoiselle Whatsername – Mornay? – marry someone?"

"You'll remember, Flora – who was the girl who played the violin?"

"The girl with the teeth – what was her name? We took her out for half-term once."

"Was it you that slipped in the bath and bled all over it, like Marat? No, that must have been the other Flora."

The time flew by. The four of them talked and laughed, and Flora hardly knew what year this was, until her mother put her head round the door to say the taxi had come.

It was like a spell breaking. Her three schoolfriends turned back into three very old ladies.

Dulcie heaved herself to her feet, huffing and puffing. "Before we go, I must have a picture of us all together – I promised the children."

Flora was startled. "You didn't tell them the truth!"

"Of course — why not? They were fascinated, and they very much want to meet you. I live with my oldest son and his family, and we're still at Merrythorpe. I hope you'll come down this summer."

"To Merrythorpe? The same one?" The sadness lifted. This had been the place she missed most from the past, and the thought of seeing it again was so blissful, it almost hurt.

"Yes, the very same one. It hasn't changed much. Some things don't." Dulcie peered through her spectacles at her phone. "Bother and blow, I've forgotten what you do! I'm sure my grandson's explained how to take a photo with this a thousand times—"

Mum came into the room in time to hear this. "I've got one of those phones. Shall I do it for you?"

"Oh, thank you! And then I'll ask someone to send you copies. Where shall we stand?"

"Let's form a group around Pete's chair," Pogo said, taking charge as usual.

Dulcie and Pogo arranged themselves on either side of Pete's chair, and Flora hung over the back.

"Say cheese, chaps!" muttered Pete. "All for one and one for all!"

Mum took the photo of three very old ladies and a lanky girl of twelve, all in fits of giggles. She seemed a little surprised by the way Flora hugged Mrs Enderby and Baroness Hooper when they left.

"We'd better leave Granny to rest," Mum said. "She's exhausted – what on earth were you all doing?"

"Oh, just catching up," Flora said. "It's incredible to be back, Mum."

Mum smoothed her hair affectionately. "It's great to have you back, darling."

"What should I be doing now?"

"What are you talking about?" Mum was laughing at her. "You're not at boarding school any more – you can do anything you like."

It was truly heavenly to have a long, hot shower in her own shower room, revelling in the gorgeous products she found in the other Flora's luggage. Goodbye, carbolic soap – and good riddance!

Afterwards, she put on her tracksuit, which was as comfortable as wearing nothing. At school it was bedtime. This time yesterday, more than seventy years in the past, she had put on a flannel dressing gown and gone to brush her teeth in the cloakroom. She had returned to the bedroom to find Pete and Dulcie dancing the cancan because it was the last night of term. It had been so recent that their voices rang in her mind's ear.

Those girls were now old and frail. But they hadn't vanished – it was important to remember that. Time passed, but there was a sort of microchip of a person's unique character that could never change.

Downstairs, the door of her grandmother's room stood open. Flora saw that Pete was now lying on the sofa, with a duvet over her legs. Dad was beside her, putting bottles of pills on a tray.

She raised her head. "Is that Flora?"

"Yes," Dad said. "But I think you should go to bed now, Mama."

"Rubbish," said Pete. "Flora, come in at once."

Flora went into the room. The old Pete glinted at her in her grandmother's hooded eyes.

"Flora and I have to do the same as we always do, on the first evening that we're together again. Tell him, darling."

This was completely new to Flora, yet somehow she knew the surprising answer. "We – we eat popcorn and watch a DVD."

"Correct," said Pete. "Please choose our entertainment."

"Mama, shouldn't you—"

"Go and make the popcorn." Pete could still rap out orders.

But Dad only laughed, and said, "You never did grow up!"

"No," Pete said. "And it's a bit late to start now, don't you think?"

If you liked

Beswitched

you'll love . . .

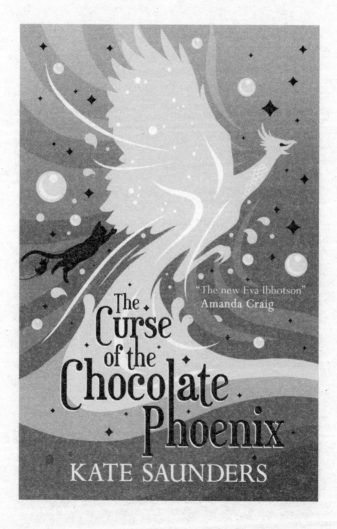

"The new Eva Ibbotson"
Amanda Craig

The
Curse
of the
Chocolate
Phoenix

KATE SAUNDERS